TOM CHATTO, SECOND MATE

The second thrilling instalment of the Tom Chatto saga.

Tom Chatto secures a berth as second officer on a liner of the Pacific Steam Navigation Company. There he discovers the difference between handling sail and relying on steam, and the difference between the world of the half deck and life on a liner with some 800 passengers. On discovering a battered windjammer in the shipping lanes, Tom is put aboard in tempestuous seas to bring the boat round Cape Horn with the Diego Ramirez rocks looming. It requires all Tom's seamanship skills to save the lives of his men.

TOM CHATTO, SECOND MATE

TOM CHATTO, SECOND MATE

by
Philip McCutchan

Magna Large Print Books
Long Preston, North Yorkshire,
England.

British Library Cataloguing in Publication Data.

McCutchan, Philip
   Tom Chatto, Second Mate.

   A catalogue record for this book is
   available from the British Library

   ISBN 0-7505-1005-6

First published in Great Britain by Weidenfeld & Nicolson,
1995

Published in Large Print August, 1996 by arrangement
with The Orion Publishing Group Limited and the
copyright holder.

Magna Large Print is an imprint of
Library Magna Books Ltd.
Printed and bound in Great Britain by
T.J. Press (Padstow) Ltd., Cornwall, PL28 8RW.

ONE

Gradually, in the years following the death of the old Queen and the ending of the war in South Africa against the Boers, a change had come over the port of Liverpool, over the whole area of the Mersey estuary. Still as busy as ever, with passengers and cargo being shifted to and from virtually every one of the world's trading ports, the scene was very different from the day Tom Chatto had reported to the boardroom of the Porter Holt Shipping Company, and as a youth of not quite seventeen had joined the old *Pass of Drumochter* as an apprentice in sail. Almost gone now was the 'forest of masts and yards' that had once characterized the Mersey, filling the berths and basins and docks of Liverpool and Birkenhead.

An era was passing; had nearly passed altogether. Now the scene was of funnels, thin and lofty, belching great plumes of smoke as the boilers were fired to produce the heads of steam that would carry the steamships out to India and China, Japan, North and South America, Australia and New Zealand.

The so-much-faster steam passages had stolen the trade away from the old windjammers, and a new breed of seaman was being born, a breed that would never know the exhilaration of plunging through blue water before a following gale, never know the droop of canvas against tall masts when lying becalmed in the Doldrums and whistling for a wind, never know the dangers of laying out along the foot ropes to take in excess sail when coming down to the High South latitudes to beat into the roaring westerlies for the east-west passage of Cape Horn.

Increasingly, the men who had started their careers in sail were deserting the windjammers for the monstrous steamships. For the sake of those careers, they had had to: there was no future left in sail. Mostly the young apprentices, having graduated to their Second Mates' Certificates, then their First Mates' and finally their Masters' Certificates of Competency, had followed the trend and, in the parlance of the day, had 'left the sea and gone into steam'.

Tom Chatto had been one of these.

'I don't need to say it, Mr Chatto,' Captain Landon had said when Tom's decision had been made, 'but I will: I shall be very sorry to lose you.'

'I'll be sorry to go, sir.'

Landon had nodded sadly. 'I know you will, young Chatto. I know you will. But there's an inevitability, and I understand very well. I wish you luck in obtaining a steamship berth.' The old man had looked away through the saloon port towards the dockside and the great warehouses and cranes and gantries of the port of London to which, on this occasion, the *Pass of Drumochter* had returned from Sydney. He seemed to be controlling a strong emotion: young Chatto was the last of his officers to remember his wife—the wife, some years younger than himself, who had sailed with him on every voyage since they had married many years before. Two years earlier she had developed appendicitis halfway across the South Pacific from Iquique in Chile to the Australian coast, and before port could be made she had died and her body in its canvas shroud had been committed to the shark-infested sea...Landon went on, 'Which steamship

9

company will you aim for?'

Tom said, 'Probably PSNC, sir.'

'Pacific Steam Navigation Company...hm. Indeed you must like the old Cape Horn and South America route! You don't think it's time for a change? Far East...or Orient Line through the Mediterranean and the Suez Canal to Australia?' Landon pondered. 'You'll probably not want the advice of an old has-been, Chatto, but if you should ask me, I'd advise a berth in some company like Royal Mail that trades over most of the world and especially the East...get a sight of China and Japan and at the same time get experience of steam and *then* apply to PSNC. They're a fine company, to be sure...but if you were to join Royal Mail as a Fourth Officer, then after a year or two PSNC might well offer you a berth as Second. Well, that's my advice and you'll take it or leave it, of course, and I'll say no more.'

'I shall certainly think about it, sir.'

'Good.' Captain Landon smiled and stood up. 'Wherever it's to be, I'll give you a reference as the best First Mate I've had for many a year.'

Years earlier, when Mr Patience, the *Pass*

of Drumochter's then First Mate, had been removed from the ship under escort to a cruiser squadron of the Queen's Navy to be charged with the murder of a French stowaway on the Chilean coast, Tom Chatto, then an apprentice, had been given a temporary berth as uncertificated Third Mate to fill a gap. Four years and many voyages around Cape Horn later, he had sat the Board of Trade examination in the Port of London and had emerged with his Second Mate's Certificate. After another two years, still under Captain Landon's command, he had obtained his First Mate's Certificate; and some eighteen months later his Master's. Not entitled to call himself a Master Mariner until he had obtained command at sea, he had progressed up the ladder to become First Mate of the *Pass of Drumochter*. This had been a very testing time; the discipline of any windjammer depended principally upon the First Mate, who, rather than the Master, the ultimate authority, had the duty of supervising the day-to-day working of the ship and her cargo. And this discipline depended in its turn on two attributes of the First Mate: the strength of his character, and when necessary the

11

strength of his fist. Patience had been a martinet and a bully; Tom Chatto was neither, but no man had ever argued with him twice or failed to obey his order.

Tom had come through. On the few occasions when his fist had been forced into play he had wondered what his father, in his quiet deanery in the west of Ireland, would have thought of his son's action. The Dean of Moyna, now a man of great age, was also a man of peace. He had not wanted Tom to go to sea in the Merchant Service. His approval would be necessary since he would be required to sign the articles of apprenticeship. It was, he had said, a rough life and not one suitable for a gentleman. But at length he had been persuaded into acceptance by the man who had aroused Tom's interest in the first place: an honorary uncle, Uncle Benjamin, who had been a student with the Dean at Trinity College in Dublin and who, having been ordained priest in the Church of Ireland, had, by some mental quirk, at once decided that the holy life was not for him after all. He had gone to sea as an apprentice in sail, and had many a yarn to tell of roaring seas, fire afloat, and ships split in half by the expansion of rice cargoes when sprung hatches had let seawater into the holds: dangers undoubtedly, but Uncle Benjamin, who now had the curious distinction of being addressed as Captain the Reverend Benjamin Brand, BA, Master Mariner, had also spoken of deep satisfaction in command at sea, with responsibility for men's lives, for valuable ships and cargo placed in the Master's trust, and of the satisfaction, when on Board of Trade Articles, of being many things rolled into one: squire, policeman, counsellor, interpreter of maritime law, judge, arbiter of every man's fate at sea, saviour in times of storm and other dangers. And Uncle Benjamin had not failed to speak, in his deep, rumbling voice, of the wider world's delights, the romantic places, the wondrous sights and experiences of all the continents from the Far East to the Americas. Tom's imagination had been fired and the fire would not go out.

'You're nothing but a stick-in-the-mud,' Benjamin Brand had said to the Dean of Moyna, taking advantage of their long friendship. 'I agree, it's not a gentleman's life, perhaps. But it's something sounder than that. It's a *man's* life. It's good fellowship as well. And it's honest, which is not to be said of all other occupations. Damn it, man, it's not as though the boy's going into trade! So give him his chance.'

The upshot had been the great, bustling port of Liverpool and the hauling out to sea with old Finney the shantyman leading the age-old capstan shanty on the fo'c'sle.

It had been hard to begin with, dropping to Fourth Officer from the lofty status of First Mate next in command after the Master: Tom had taken Landon's advice and had sought and found, with his recommendation, a berth with the Royal Mail Steam Packet Company. Appointed to the steamship *Bulolo* lying in Birkenhead, he had taken his leave of Captain Landon and taken the train from Euston Station to Lime Street, his new Royal Mail uniform packed into his seachest in the guard's van. He had parted from Landon with genuine sorrow; Landon had been his instructor in seamanship, in ship-handling, in navigation and the ways of the sea; and finally he had become a friend, one in whom Tom had absolute trust. Now he felt very much on his own, travelling back to the familiarity

14

of Liverpool but into the as yet strange new world of steam. Leaving the old *Pass of Drumochter* he had had a strong feeling that he and Landon would not meet again. In due time this was to be proved true: the news was to reach him while on passage home from Japanese ports that the old windjammer had been lost with all hands in the course of a violent passage of Cape Horn when she had been dismasted in high winds and heavy seas, had sprung her cargo hatches and was left a drifting, helpless wreck to be driven hard and fast on to the dreaded Diego Ramirez rocks a little south-west of the Horn. In this there was just one consolation: Landon had been an old man, on the verge of seventy, and would soon have been forced ashore to live out a lonely existence divorced from all that had made his life worth while.

Aboard the *Bulolo*, a handsome, two-masted, single-funnelled vessel of 6500 tons, Tom as Fourth Officer kept a watch at sea as assistant to the First Officer, the senior watch-keeper. He learned the differences of steam, the reliance on the 'black gang' below instead of on clean canvas and fresh winds. Compared with sail, it was easy enough once he had got accustomed to engine-room telegraphs in place of orders shouted into gales for the trimming of canvas and the hauling of the braces to catch the wind. He had to accustom himself to a new breed of seafarers: the engineers, the greasers, the firemen who toiled with shovelfuls of coal in the heat and squalor of the boiler rooms, men working like devils from hell before the glowing, red-hot furnaces. These were men for whom one was bound to have respect for their sheer stamina and guts when working in appalling conditions in the searing, airless heat of the Suez Canal and the Red Sea, conditions so severe that heatstroke was a fairly common occurrence and men would be brought to the upper deck to lie between blocks of ice from the refrigeration that kept the fresh meat in the meat rooms fit to eat. At the same time, to a seaman from the windjammers, there was a strong feeling of repugnance for the new breed that produced the clouds of filthy, black smoke, the smuts and choking fumes of which blew over the bridge watchkeepers when there was a following wind, sullying clean white uniforms and obscuring the lookout ahead.

Tom had to become accustomed to

the continual wearing of uniform; in the windjammers at sea, any rig would do, the more comfortable the better. And he had to become used to another new breed: the passengers. In a windjammer there were no passengers; there was work for everyone aboard, and no idlers. Tom, as time went on, found that passengers could bring dangers. Not dangers to the ship, but dangers to a young officer's career. Families sailing to the Far East often enough brought daughters with them, young women in a strange environment only too ready to be impressed by gold-braided uniforms which, when added to the glamour of Eastern waters and moon-filled nights, could lead quickly to events not approved of by shipowners. Many a liner career had foundered when a course had been set in that direction. The temptations were hard to resist.

Three years with Royal Mail saw Tom Chatto with a Second Officer's berth; that, and the bonus, after four years' service, of a voyage off in lieu of leave not taken in the interval. Tom signed off Articles in Liverpool, and took the night ferry across to the North Wall in Dublin, where he entrained at Westland Row for the remote west of Ireland and the deanery at Moyna.

It was strange to be back after long absence. His father had grown frail, and was still rather disapproving of a sailor son. Tom's brother Philip, now a captain in the Connaught Rangers and on leave from the military camp at the Curragh, was inclined to be somewhat superior, metaphorically looking down his nose at a roughneck. Brother Edward the parson was, thankfully, not at Moyna, busying himself with the old biddies of his parish in County Galway. But Tom had a good friend at court: Uncle Benjamin still hale and hearty, staying again with the Dean and keen to hear all Tom had to tell about his life.

'Are you intending to stay with Royal Mail?' Uncle Benjamin asked.

Tom was uncertain. 'I'm not sure yet. They're a good company to work for. Good ships, good conditions...'

'But—there is a but?'

'Well—yes, there is, Uncle Benjamin. I—'

'You always hankered after PSNC, Tom.'

'Yes.'

'But you took old Landon's advice. It was good advice.' Uncle Benjamin took up the whiskey decanter that stood on a small table between their chairs. 'The sun, I think, is well enough over the foreyard. So you'll take a little of your father's whiskey, and so shall I.' He poured two stiff measures. Whiskey was ever on tap in Ireland's west; in Benjamin Brand's own house a barrel of it stood ready in the hall for anyone to help him or herself, Irishwomen being mostly as ready to tap it as were the men. Tom recalled that Uncle Benjamin had a female cousin, known as the Mountains of Mourne on account of her great girth, who was accustomed when staying away to take with her a number of stone hot-water bottles filled with whiskey as a standby just in case the supply should inadvertently run out... Uncle Benjamin went on, 'Landon said, as I understand, that the time would come when you might try for a berth on the South American run?'

Tom nodded. 'I think I should have a fair chance, Uncle Benjamin. You probably know that PSNC has always regarded Porter Holt as a good supplier of sail-trained officers.'

'Yes, indeed I do know that. But what's so attractive about that particular run, Tom?'

Tom shrugged. 'Hard to say, really... except that I got so used to it in sail and I liked the countries—Chile and the Argentine—when I got the chance to go ashore. We put in to Valparaiso quite often for storm damage repairs as well as discharging and loading cargo, which meant a week or more in port. I got to know people...made good friends.' He paused, frowning. 'All those years...I felt more at home there than I ever did in the East. China, Japan, Singapore—I found it claustrophobic in a sense. Too many coolies, too many junks, too many sampans, it was like a madhouse more often than not, trying to enter and leave the various ports. Too much native chatter, and everything seemed to run on bribery. The Chief Officer of the *Bulolo* was always being approached by shippers, some sort of jiggery-pokery with the cargo.'

'Which he refused, of course.'

'Of course. But it left a nasty taste. Danger, too.'

'A knife in the back, in the Street of the Swinging Tit?'

20

Tom laughed. 'Exactly! It was always on the cards if you didn't play ball.'

'Quite. The sea's no easy life—well, you know that by now. Any other reason?' Uncle Benjamin cocked an eyebrow quizzically, and Tom flushed. He took a mouthful of whiskey. Uncle Benjamin had an uncanny way of penetrating minds, and now there was a twinkle in his rather bloodshot eye. Tom decided to come out with the truth.

'I met someone aboard the *Bulolo*. A passenger.'

'Ah. A young woman passenger, should I take it?'

'Yes. Travelling with an uncle—'

'Another uncle, bless my soul, shoving his oar in—'

'Just a trip, seeing the world—'

'And she lives in South America?'

'Yes, the Argentine. Her father's an *estancia* owner, beef—'

'She's Argentinian?'

'Yes,' Tom said defensively. 'Her name is Dolores Pontarena.'

Uncle Benjamin went off into a gale of laughter as though unable to stop. When he had calmed down he gasped, 'Well, bless my soul, young Tom, what your father's going to say I really don't know.

First I am instrumental in sending you off to sea, and now I look like being instrumental in furthering your designs upon an Argentinian whose father peddles beef. Instrumental because, you see, I have a very good friend who happens to be a director of PSNC, and if that's truly your considered wish, I shall take much pleasure in writing to him before your leave's up.'

'Really, Benjamin! A—a *dago!*'

'But probably wealthy. There's a deal of money in beef.'

'It's not suitable for Tom.'

'Not suitable for yourself, you mean. And not suitable for the Connaught Rangers?'

'Don't fool, Benjamin.' The Dean shifted irritably in his chair. 'If this is serious—*if*—she'll make him leave the sea.'

'My dear old friend, you didn't want him to go in the first place.'

'Perhaps not. But neither do I wish him to leave this country to live in the Argentine on—what is it?—a beef station.'

'I wouldn't look too far ahead if I were you. It's perhaps no more than an infatuation and his ship will rarely be long in Buenos Aires. First love seldom lasts.

The point is, he genuinely wants a berth in PSNC, and in my opinion as a seaman he couldn't do better.'

'You're a confounded interferer,' the Dean of Moyna said pettishly, and Captain Benjamin Brand nodded his large head as if in total agreement.

Three weeks later Tom Chatto left the deanery for Dublin and the Mersey to face the board of directors of the Pacific Steam Navigation Company at their Liverpool headquarters. Three days later, largely thanks to Captain Benjamin Brand and the previously written testimony of Captain Landon, Tom was appointed Second Officer of the company's liner *Orvega* of 8648 gross tonnage, soon to be outward bound for Valparaiso in Chile and en route ports.

TWO

Captain Matheson Fullbright, Master of the *Orvega*, was, Tom thought, well-named. He was a big man of full stature, inclined to roundness of body

23

and with extraordinarily bright blue eyes, very penetrating eyes as he looked his new Second Officer up and down. Captain Fullbright had rejoined the ship from leave this day, sailing day for South American ports. 'Now then, Mr Chatto,' he said to Tom, 'First Mate in sail as I understand, and now with some years' experience of steam.'

'Yes, sir.'

Fullbright rubbed a horny hand over his chin. 'Tell me, Mr Chatto. How do you find the sea now?'

'Sir?'

'I mean, Mr Chatto, which do you prefer—sail or steam?'

Tom thought for a moment. 'I like the comfort of steam, sir. But in a sense it's no longer the sea.'

'Nothing to fight against?'

'I think that's it, sir. There's not the same satisfaction in a safe arrival.'

'A profound thought, Mr Chatto.' Tom was uncertain whether or not the Captain was being sardonic; but Fullbright went on, 'My officers have mostly taken backward looks to more seamanlike days, as I do myself. I think we shall get along together, Mr Chatto. But I take issue with you on one point: you'll find plenty to fight against in steam, though it may not be against the sea. Look down there.'

They were on the bridge, standing together in the starboard wing. Below, the shore gangways were rigged to the embarkation deck and the passengers were beginning to straggle up from the dockside littered with items of cargo from the warehouses, with cranes and shouting stevedores wielding dangerous-looking cargo hooks, and with taxis and horse-drawn cabs that had brought the passengers from the railway station.

'Well, Mr Chatto? Passengers—d'you see them?'

'Yes, sir—'

'Danger! Watch your step with them. They're unpredictable. They're also a damn nuisance to a seaman, though I'm not to be quoted on that to the board. They get in the way, Mr Chatto, and they expect young officers to be polite even when they feel like murder. But of course you've encountered the breed in Royal Mail.'

'Yes, sir.'

'Remember this: passengers, especially as it happens first-class passengers, or should I say, as the stewards do, passengers travelling first class—you'll appreciate the difference—tend to mark their brains "Not Wanted On Voyage" and consign them to the baggage room. Bear that in mind when dealing with them, that's my advice.' Captain Fullbright changed tack. 'You have your courses laid for Funchal, Mr Chatto?'

'Yes, sir. And all chart corrections entered from the Admiralty Notices to Mariners.' As Second Officer, navigation would be Tom's responsibility under the Captain. Fullbright nodded and as the purser came up the bridge ladder and saluted Tom was dismissed. He went below to the embarkation deck and stood by the head of the ladder for a word with an assistant purser and the ship's master-at-arms who were checking the passengers aboard before passing them on to the care of the hovering stewards. Tom watched a mixed bunch making their way up the gangway. These were the steerage passengers; next would come the second class, and finally the first class who, being last to embark, would have the shorter wait before the tugs hauled the liner off the wall to head outwards for the Skerries and the turn south for St George's Channel.

The steerage passengers were mostly families, father and mother and excited, ill-clad children. Tom wondered what their purpose might be in going to South America; they had the look of emigrants, though what work they could expect to find in the Argentine or Chile was beyond comprehension. Perhaps anything was better than unemployment in Britain, or employment on starvation wages. There were a few who appeared to be on their own, both men and women.

One in particular, a man who appeared to be in his sixties, emaciated and sick-looking but yet truculent, stood out.

Tom watched, in growing astonishment as recognition dawned. As he watched, the man looked up. Their eyes met. Older now, though not as old in fact as he looked, the man was Patience, once First Mate of the *Pass of Drumochter,* last seen being taken into the custody of the British Navy on a charge of murder.

On the first night at sea, neither passengers nor ship's officers dressed for dinner. On subsequent nights Tom would shift into mess dress, narrow-cut trousers, starched shirt and bum-freezer with the two gold stripes of his rank on the cuffs. Also on that first night, the seat at the head of the Captain's table stood empty: in coastal waters, the Master remained on the bridge, not leaving its vicinity until his command was clear away to the open sea and the wide waters of the Atlantic.

Tom, at the head of his own table in the first-class saloon, made conversation with the passengers. On his right was a man who turned out to be a bank manager in the employ of Barclays Bank, a Mr Tomkin. Beside him sat Mrs Tomkin, a stringy woman with a sour face, probably a potential complainer; next to her a spotty son aged about nineteen by Tom's guess. On the left, a retired army officer and his wife, a Lieutenant and Mrs Tidy. Tidy, Tom was informed, had been a lieutenant and quartermaster promoted from the ranks of the Lincolnshire Regiment before retirement; he was an unusual person to find in the first class, perhaps, but it turned out that his wife had inherited a legacy and this voyage was a once-in-a-lifetime indulgence—to visit a son in South America. Tidy was a garrulous man, his wife complementing his garrulity by remaining totally silent after a first nervous pleased-to-meet-you in response to Tom's greeting. The others at the table included a Mrs Westby, a pleasant widow with a daughter about the same age as the Tomkin youth; an Englishman, by name Bolsover, returning from extended leave to his job as manager of an *estancia* in the Argentine but currently going all the way to Valparaiso in pursuit of his employer's Chilean interests, who looked as though he enjoyed his drink. There was also an American, a citizen, as he announced loudly, of the 'good ole USA', his name, equally loudly announced, being Percival J. Bunce ('Call me Percy'). His occupation did not emerge but he could have been a salesman travelling on his company's business. The more important of the passengers would be at the purser's or the Chief Officer's tables; the most important, or the most valuable to the Line, would be at the Captain's table.

That night there were the usual casualties as the liner met the first of the Atlantic weather off the Old Head of Kinsale. The first to leave the table was the spotty Tomkin, clutching a hand to his mouth and weaving a staggering run across the tilting deck of the saloon.

He was followed by his mother, and a little later by his father. Next was Mrs Westby; the daughter weathered the motion, exchanging a grimace with Tom. Then Mrs Tidy clambered to her feet.

'Pardon me,' she said, and ran.

The lieutenant and quartermaster said apologetically, 'Women!'

Tom grinned. When the pudding arrived only Tidy, the Westby daughter, Bolsover and Percival J. Bunce were left; and for the first time in his life Tom heard an American actually say, 'Gee whiz.'

Tom lifted an eyebrow quizzically.

'This sweet. Sure is good.' The pudding, which consisted of something in custard, was almost literally lapped up. Percival J. Bunce, wiping his lips with his napkin, certainly didn't suffer from seasickness. But the rest of the meal passed in an awkward silence, the American having left the table to progress towards the bar. Oddly, Lieutenant Tidy, in the absence of his silent wife, seemed to dry up. It was possibly her very silence that caused his garrulity. As for Tom, he found it difficult to initiate a conversation with passengers. He still hankered after the free-and-easy talk of a windjammer's half-deck or saloon, the easy flow between shipmates with a shared interest.

He turned in early, to get some sleep before his bridge watch at 0400 next morning.

Sleep was slow to come. Tom's mind revolved around that unexpected sight of Patience. What could have happened, how had the man skated from under a well-authenticated charge of murder? There had never been any subsequent news, not even when the windjammer had discharged cargo in Valparaiso. If Captain Landon had been informed privately he had never divulged anything; Tom believed the old man had wanted nothing more than to leave an unfortunate episode behind him and had therefore closed his mind to it. But those far-off events on the South Chilean coast were vivid still in Tom's mind. The stowaway, the Frenchman Paul Chardonnet, alias Fontanet, himself a confessed murderer of a bullying mate in the ship from which he had deserted, had made his escape ashore after putting the *Pass of Drumochter* aground on rocks off the treacherous coast to leeward. Search parties had been organized, with Mr Patience in charge of one of them. The Frenchman had eventually been run to earth and Patience had shot him in cold blood after he had surrendered. Patience had sworn he had never heard any words of surrender; but the seamen of the landing party had been positive.

Tom himself remembered the words clearly: 'It is an inhospitable and terrible country, this,' the Frenchman had called out. 'Me, I have had enough. I surrender.' That was clear enough; and all hands had known very well that Patience had had it in for the stowaway. When the grounding of the windjammer was seen from the navigating bridges of the 14th Cruiser Squadron of the British Fleet, proceeding north along the Chilean coast from Cape Horn, boats had been sent. Captain Landon had had no option but to transfer Patience into naval custody for handing over to the authorities in Valparaiso, together with depositions from the men of the landing party.

What had gone wrong?

And why was Patience going back to South America?

After the sighting on the gangway, Tom had checked with the steerage passenger list in the purser's office. Ainsworth, the purser, had noted his interest in the list and had asked if he could help. Tom gave him the name: Patience. 'I can't find him in the list. But I know I saw him.'

Ainsworth reached across. 'Let's have a look.' He scanned all three lists, first, second and steerage; there was no Patience. 'What interests you about the man?' he asked.

'I think I've met him before, that's all.' With Patience still at large, it was at least possible that somehow or other he had avoided the charge—or as Percival J. Bunce might have said, beaten the rap. If so, then to speak of murder could be actionable for slander. On the other hand, Patience might have escaped from a Chilean gaol, been on the run for all those past years. But if that was the case, then surely he wouldn't be going back to anywhere on the South American continent?

For now, it had to remain a mystery. It was just possible that Patience—whom Tom was convinced knew he'd been recognized—would make contact in due course. Until he was more certain as to how the land lay, Tom was not going to cause ructions with his new company.

He told Ainsworth he had probably been mistaken after all.

In the morning watch, from 0400 to 0800, the wind increased from the west. The *Orvega,* before turning south, was making her westing and butting into an increasing swell. Looking down from the bridge, watching the deckhands busy with the hoses and squeegees, Tom saw few passengers about. But there were always those in any liner who made a fetish of walking a set number of times around the boat or promenade decks daily, and this morning was no exception. Percival J. Bunce was on the march, lurching to the ship's movement as the bows dipped under and rose again in a series of short jerks. At times the American seemed to rise a few inches into the air, feet scrabbling, before thumping back as the deck rose to meet him. He shouted cheery greetings to the deckhands. 'Morning, morning, you guys. Say, this is the air that freshens you up, nothing like it on God's earth, right? Well, gee whiz.' This latter exclamation was due to the emergence of the Westby daughter from a weather door that banged shut behind her on the wind.

The American made a beeline for her. She didn't look as though she welcomed it. Bunce was probably a womanizer: Tom had summed him up the night before as Bouncy Bunce. He had elicited that Bunce was unmarried but eager and noted that eyes had been made across the tablecloth. Miss Westby had not responded, keeping her eyes down. Mr Bunce, aged around forty, was too old for her even if she had been interested; too old and too brash. As, this morning, the girl made rather fast for another weather door giving access below, the westerly wind brought the beseeching sound of Mr Bunce's voice: 'Call me Percy.'

Over the succeeding days the weather moderated. By this time the *Orvega* had altered course to port and was steaming on a SSE track to make a landfall at Funchal in Madeira, her first coaling port. Although, with the wind still westerly, she had developed a fairly pronounced roll, the first-class passengers had got their sea legs enough for them to attend the mealtimes. Lieutenant and Quartermaster Tidy was as garrulous as ever, yarning away about his late regiment and how, when on foreign service in India, the natives had spent their time doing their best to pinch his stores but how he had always managed to outwit them—this latter information was accompanied by a wink and a nudge that almost caused Tom to spill his soup. Mrs Tidy remained as silent as ever, seeming to concentrate on her soup, drinking it with a painfully genteel absence of sound as it slid down her throat. Tom, thinking of the Dean's uninhibited slurping as he enjoyed a good Irish broth, found the silent absorption overdone and rather nauseating.

Leaving the saloon after dinner, Tom buttonholed Bolsover, the returning *estancia* manager. 'Would you care to join me in the lounge for coffee, Mr Bolsover?'

'Don't mind if I do—thanks.' They found two adjacent armchairs. A lounge steward brought coffee, handed sugar and fresh cream-fresh cream from the refrigerated stores that would soon be exhausted and would be replaced by evaporated milk. Tom got Bolsover on to a discussion of *estancias,* which turned out to be his pet subject in any case. Bolsover had been for many years in the Argentine and turned out to be a prolific source of useful information. Yes, indeed, he knew the name Pontarena, he knew it very well and he knew Señor Pontarena also.

'Rich,' he said with a touch of envy. 'Very, very rich. About the biggest bloody estate in the Argentine. Know him yourself, do you, eh?'

'No. I've met his daughter. Dolores... Dolores Pontarena.' Tom was still young enough—just—to get satisfaction from speaking aloud the name of what he regarded as his *inamorata*; but on this occasion he was corrected by the *estancia* manager. 'Dolores *de Catalan* Solana Pontarena in full, by the Lord God!' He tapped the side of his nose in a gesture reminiscent of Lieutenant Tidy's nudge. 'Aristocratic Spanish grandma who in fact didn't go much on Conrado—Conrado Pontarena. Not out of the top drawer, you see. He's rich, as I said. But he's also a bastard, none bigger. Drives his hands—they all loathe his guts and he's said to have fingers in any number of shady pies, but if you ever repeat that, young man, I'll be having *your* guts for garters. Understood?'

Tom laughed good-naturedly. 'Understood,' he said. 'You have my word on it.'

'I reckoned you a man of your word the first time I set eyes on you in the saloon. And I believed you'd give it or I wouldn't have spoken. Just a word to the wise, see—or should I say a word in time, if you get me.' Bolsover paused, drank some coffee, lit a cigar and looked Tom up and down as he offered his cigar case. 'Got an eye on the girl by any chance?'

'Well...'

Bolsover reached across and put a hand on his knee, chuckling. 'It's all right, say no more. I don't know Señorita Pontarena, but I believe she's an eyeful and a really nice girl with it. That's what they say when we managers get together in B.A. But it's also said the old bugger'll never let her go, and any hopeful lad hanging around is as likely as not to get a bullet up the arse.' He wagged a finger. 'The interior of the Argentine is still pretty wild and woolly, and the estate owners are pretty much the law, such as it is.'

Tom didn't care for the sound of it, but put it down perhaps largely to exaggeration and envy of a rich *estancia* owner. They chatted on for a while and when later they were joined by Mrs Westby and her daughter Tom failed to notice the passing minutes.

'Mr Chatto.'

The voice next morning was sharp, also somewhat pettish. Tom looked up towards the bridge. Three gold stripes loomed to his two: the Chief Officer, short, red-haired, fat as a barrel. And very, very important in his own estimation, which went a long way. Where Captain Matheson Fullbright appeared human and had a sense of humour, Mr Joseph Forster did not and had not. Obsessed by the importance of his position and by the likelihood of a command within a year or so, he was an inveterate picker of nits.

'Yes, sir?'

Mr Forster glowered. 'Don't stand there saying yes, sir. Come up to the bridge immediately.'

Tom climbed the ladder. The Captain, he noted, was in the chart room in the rear of the bridge with the side port open. Mr Forster was about to be (loudly) efficient.

'Mr Chatto, one presumes you're able to tell the time?'

Murder might well be worth while. 'Yes, sir,' Tom said.

'Good, excellent.' Mr Forster rubbed his hands together briskly. 'In that case...Mr Chatto, you are no doubt fully aware that deck officers are expected, by the Company's rules and regulations, to be cleared away from the public rooms and spaces by 2200 hours? I am correct in assuming that, am I not?'

Of course you are, daft ha'porth. 'Yes, sir.'

Mr Forster brought out a silver turnip-shaped watch and appeared to study it. In indignant tones he said, 'Then why, may one ask, were you in the lounge with passengers at *two minutes past* the permitted hour last night?'

Tom smiled icily. 'I admit the charge, sir. I apologize. I trust the enormity didn't keep you awake all night. Sin, according to my father, a clergyman, does have that effect both on the sinner and the sinned against.'

Forster reddened and spluttered something. Tom took this as dismissal; he turned away down the ladder.

Tom didn't overhear the next act; nor was he intended to. Captain Fullbright left the chart room and went below to the Master's deck and his own accommodation. Then he whistled up the voicepipe to the bridge.

'Ah, Mr Forster. Perhaps you'd be good enough to come to my day-cabin. Yes, now, please. *Thank* you.'

Fullbright replaced the voicepipe cover. There was a knock at his door. The Chief Officer entered, his cap beneath his left arm.

'You wished to see me, sir.'

'Yes. Mr Forster...you were my Chief Officer on the last voyage and I would have thought you understood my ways better than you have just shown.'

Forster reddened again but remained silent.

'I will not have you reprimand any of my officers or senior ratings when their subordinates, in this case the helmsman and others, are within hearing. Is that quite clear?'

'Captain Fullbright, I did not—'

'And you will also not answer back to me, Mr Forster, nor will you attempt to argue with your Captain.' Fullbright's jaw came forward pugnaciously. Not in the normal way a pugnacious man, Fullbright's personal opinion of his Chief Officer was that the man was a puffed-up bag of

41

bullshit who had been lucky to reach his present rank as second-in-command of the ship. He dismissed Forster and then gave a heavy sigh. He would dearly have liked to queer Forster's pitch for the command he would most likely get, but he was a fair-minded man and could never allow himself to behave in such a fashion without overriding cause. And Forster was a good seaman. That was really what counted, after all. Fullbright, up early that morning and on the bridge following a report that there was some difficulty in the engine room, nothing really serious, rang for his steward and told the man to run his bath, after which he would have breakfast. In his cabin, not the first-class saloon. Passengers were a bit much so early in any master mariner's day.

THREE

Landfall for Funchal in Madeira was made five days after the *Orvega* had cleared away from Liverpool Bay. At Funchal the ship would coal: the Chief Engineer would

42

take 850 tons of good Welsh coal into his bunkers. This would be a time of coal dust that would penetrate every nook and cranny of the ship, being sucked down the ventilators, or such as would need to be left open to admit air, to spread filth throughout the cabins and public rooms. The work for the hands would be cruel: bag after bag to be brought inboard from lighters and manhandled to the chutes to cascade down into the bunkers.

There would be a twenty-four-hour stay in Funchal; mostly the passengers would go ashore to spend the night in hotels, but this would not apply to the steerage, where the men and women and children, unable to afford this luxury, would be left aboard to suffer the filth, the heat and the inconvenience, with the ubiquitous coal dust getting beneath their clothing and into the stowages provided in the twelve-berth cabins low down in the ship, mostly below the waterline.

Tom had seen the conditions, when making inspection rounds, before they were worsened by the coaling. He found those conditions as primitive as any half-deck, or even fo'c'sle, in the windjammers. In the Royal Mail's vessels no steerage passengers had been carried, though some of the ships, ones in which he had not himself served, carried coolie accommodation. In Tom's view, the steerage accommodation was probably little better than that accorded the coolies. The sexes were strictly segregated in male and female cabins, the younger children all being berthed with the women. There was scarcely room to swing a cat, even to undress in comfort, while the washing facilities were rudimentary to say the least. The result was foetid air, heavy with the stench of sweat, unwashed bodies and dirty clothing; it was painful to take a breath and Tom, escaping as soon as possible to the upper deck, wondered how human beings could bear to pass whole nights in the stifling, smelly atmosphere with nothing but a small portion, set right aft above the screws, of the lowest open deck in which to find air and some room to move.

On his inspections, he saw no sign of Patience; he began to wonder if, after all, he could have been mistaken. But he did not believe so.

As navigator, Tom was on the bridge for the Funchal arrival along with the Captain and the First Officer, Charles Fordyce. The Chief Officer stood in the eyes of the ship, standing by for letting go the anchor on orders from the bridge.

Tom used the azimuth circle on the magnetic compass, checking his bearings as the ship, with engines at slow ahead, inched up towards the anchorage as allotted by signal from the harbour master. When Tom sang out that they were approaching their position Captain Fullbright stepped to the front of the bridge and raised his anchor flag: green, for the starboard anchor. In the bow, Forster did likewise.

'In position, sir,' Tom called. The Captain's hand came down. Forster lowered his sharply and called out, *'Let go!'* The brake was taken off the windlass by the carpenter and the cable roared out from the cable locker in a red cloud of dust, bouncing from the protective metal plates laid along the planking of the fo'c'sle-head. Forster, leaning out over the starboard side, kept an eye on the cable markings.

As the third shackle was seen, Forster, with a lifted hand, stopped the cable's outrush. 'Three shackles on deck, sir,' he called through his megaphone.

'Thank you, Mr Forster. Secure when she has her cable, if you please.'

'Aye, aye, sir.' The barrel-like figure fussed about the fo'c'sle, issuing unnecessary orders to seamen who knew their jobs well enough. As the ship came up to her cable, he ordered the slips to be put on and then dismissed the cable party to go below for their breakfasts.

On the bridge, Chief Engineer Harrison reported in person to the Captain.

'Good morning, Chief.' Fullbright raised an eyebrow. 'Not trouble, I hope?'

'A bit of difficulty, sir. Nothing too serious, but some shoreside assistance may be needed. Same as before...the low-pressure valve spindle's playing up.'

'Is a delay likely, Chief?'

Harrison shrugged. 'If it should break, then yes. But otherwise not too long, I fancy.'

'Can you estimate?'

'Depends on the shore,' Harrison said. 'Portuguese labour...I don't know.' He shrugged.

'All right, Chief. Keep me informed, won't you?' Chief Engineers were all the same, didn't like committing themselves. Any protracted delay could throw out the schedule, possibly all the way to Rio, the Plate and beyond, around Cape Horn to Valparaiso, unless time could be made up en route. Steamships ran always to schedule. Not for the first time, Fullbright thought back nostalgically to his days in sail. In those days schedules were there to be broken into smithereens. The weather invariably saw to that, weather being unpredictable. But weather didn't bother steamships too much. Engine rooms did.

The port authorities came aboard. The purser, closeted with them and the Captain, produced the ship's papers: bills of lading, cargo manifests, customs' forms, passenger lists. With them came the port medical officer who was taken to the surgery to consult with the ship's doctor and grant pratique.

He did not grant pratique. While they were talking, a steward came to report a woman sick in the steerage. The eyes of the two doctors met. Dr Murphy, ship's doctor, asked for symptoms.

'Feverish, sir. Sweating, like. And head-ache.'

'I'll take a look,' Murphy said. The

47

shore doctor went with him into the foul atmosphere of the steerage accommodation deck. The woman looked ghastly and had been sick. At once the shore doctor said, 'Isolation, please.'

'Of course. But I don't believe it's anything serious.'

'Your diagnosis, Doctor?'

'I can't say for sure yet. I'll have her taken to the sickbay and then—we'll see.'

'No risks, please, for Funchal.' The Portuguese doctor was already in a tizzy, was going to play safe. Obviously. The sick woman, in her thirties but looking twice that, was removed to the sickbay. Dr Murphy made such tests as he could. He believed it to be nothing more than influenza, brought aboard in Liverpool. An epidemic in the steerage accommodation would be a confoundedly inconvenient business, but there was nothing for the little Portuguese to get in a state about. Nevertheless he did get in a state and made his pronouncement without ado.

'The diagnosis is not confirmed in my mind, Doctor. The disease could be many things. The ship is *contaminado*. There will be no pratique, and no one is to leave the ship.'

'What,' Chief Engineer Harrison demanded, 'is to happen about my repair?'

Fullbright shrugged. 'You know the rules, Chief. No contact between ship and shore. We'll have to cope with our own difficulties. I'll make representations to the Consul, of course. And I'll report by wireless to Liverpool. But I doubt if all that'll do any good—you know these people.'

'Jacks in office,' Harrison said disgustedly. A moment later the purser knocked and entered the day cabin: the passengers, kept aboard like prisoners, willy-nilly, throughout the coaling operation, were going to be restive.

Fullbright gave a short laugh. 'Restive's probably an understatement, Purser! But I'm afraid passengers are the least of my worries at the moment. Have you spoken to the chief steward?'

'Yes, sir. He's worried about his supplies. Fresh fruit, vegetables...anyway, he and I will see what we can do about keeping the passengers occupied, keep their minds off their woes.'

'Good. I don't envy your staff when the siege of the office starts.'

'It's started already, sir,' the purser gloomed.

A purser's lot was always a hard one. In Ainsworth's jaundiced view after some thirty years at sea, eight hundred and fifty passengers meant eight hundred and fifty silly questions per day throughout the voyage.

There was nothing silly enough. It drove many pursers to drink, and the evening sessions in bar and cabins were ever the best hours of a purser's day. On this occasion there was a seething mass of complainers filling the lobby outside the counter of the office. What use was the doctor if he couldn't override the damned natives? Why should a Portuguese doctor be allowed to get away with a nonsensical restriction on British liberty—the word had spread like lightning, as things do at sea, that the sick woman was suffering from nothing more serious than influenza? On the other hand, there were those who feared that she might in fact be suffering from something else and if so it was the Line's responsibility to get them off the ship and into disease-free accommodation ashore. The ship could then ride out the epidemic at anchor and re-embark them when it was all over. It would, of course, be PSNC's responsibility to pay their hotel bills and other resultant expenses. In vain Ainsworth tried to explain the totality of no pratique. The passengers milled about, some of the women tearful, the children yelling until the fathers threatened thick ears.

Bedlam, Ainsworth called it.

He retreated to his private office leading off the main office and spoke again with the chief steward. Tombola would be organized in the first- and second-class lounges. There would be the usual deck games: quoits, table tennis, races. The chief steward fancied that he might be able to get a stewards' concert party together for an impromptu performance. Every voyage customarily produced a stewards' concert for the passengers, but this was normally put on towards the end of the voyage, just before the Valparaiso arrival. A favourite ploy of the stewards was to get the passengers to join in a singsong, sometimes a chorus with doubtful words.

Coaling went ahead. This necessitated no direct physical contact with the shore. The

Portuguese remained aboard their lighters, the ship's crew remained on their own decks; disease could not be spread by bags of coal. Overridingly, the economy of Funchal relied on the provision of coal and the Portuguese knew on which side their bread was buttered. After much shilly-shallying, fresh provisions were allowed aboard, such also being a vital feature of the local economy, though in the circumstances the price went up, a fact of life that the purser and chief steward were obliged to accept. The passengers lined the rails along the boat and promenade decks and gloomed towards the shore, towards the steep sides of Pico Ruivo rising to more than six thousand feet under a blue sky. They left the rails when a string of deep-laden coal lighters approached the ship and made fast alongside as the *Orvega's* deckhands, under the bosun, threw down securing lines. Soon the ship lay under a virtual blanket of coal dust.

The chief steward had achieved success with the concert party: after that night's dinner, the first-class passengers assembled in the lounge and, following an announcement from the purser, the entertainment began. There were clever takeoffs of various personalities, one of them being the Chief Officer, he being not present. It all went down well; important ladies and gentlemen from the Captain's table laughed in the right places, and applauded. Tom was sitting with Lieutenant and Mrs Tidy, the Westby mother and daughter, and Percival J. Bunce. The latter thought it all great, and said so enthusiastically. He'd never before, he said, travelled in a limey ship; he'd always thought a limey ship would be unendurable, filled with stuffed-shirt limey stuck-ups, but now he saw his error. He joined in wholeheartedly with a number laid on for the passengers' participation, a simple and many-times-repeated ditty, or couplet, led by the stewards at an increasing tempo:

'She sits and shines
And shines and sits...'

Mrs Tidy's face became as red as a beetroot, and for the first time she was heard to utter, 'Well, really, I call that *scandalous*, really I do!'

The complaints, next day, reached the Captain. He sent for the purser. 'I trust

I'm a broad-minded man, Purser, but it just won't do. It might be all right in the steerage...but if the show's to be put on in the second class, it'll have to be edited. There's such a thing as taste, you know.'

Ainsworth apologized. The Captain grinned. 'The men it was who complained to me. On behalf of their ladies...and do you know, I felt half inclined to ask how it was that the good ladies had ever heard the word.' He turned to his desk. 'Well, now. The Chief's had no success with his repair job—they refuse to put any men aboard, so we leave with a shipboard botch-up—no damn alternative until we reach Rio or the Plate. I'll want wireless messages sent to Liverpool.' He produced a sheet of Company's writing paper. 'That's my draft. See that the wireless office sends it without delay, if you please. And here's another for onward transmission to the agents in Rio...'

During the following morning watch the deckhands were busy with hoses and squeegees, cleaning down the open decks. The stewards and stewardesses had their work cut out in the cabins and alleyways and public rooms. In the steerage, the passengers had to make do with their own efforts: steerage passengers didn't rate stewards. There was sickness to add to squalor. The doctor's diagnosis was confirmed in his own mind: influenza. Not too serious, though there could be complications. Even without complications, it was a terrible enough business in those confined, smelly decks. There was certainly no room in the ship's small sickbay for the bed cases; Dr Murphy and his nursing sister, Anne Moloney, did their best, working all hours to bring some sort of comfort to the worst afflicted. The womenfolk who had not yet succumbed were roped in as nursing aides, and did good work, most of them, in holding basins to catch vomit, attending so far as possible to bodily functions, feeding, wiping down sweat-streaked brows, and looking after the children.

Anne Moloney worked under difficulties: the difficulties due to the fact that, simply, she was a woman, and young and attractive. She was the only woman from outside the steerage to come into that section of the ship. She was also the only woman to be admitted to the male cabins: the segregation was otherwise total, and was enforced by the ship's master-at-arms, ex-Royal Navy where he had been chief of ship's police in a battleship, and by the prowling, vigilant nightwatchmen, one of whom at least had been a colour sergeant of the Royal Marine Light Infantry and in his day had been the terror of the parade ground in Forton Barracks at Gosport in Hampshire.

Anne Moloney entered the steerage as an angel of mercy and as a pretty girl to be stalked by sex-hungry men. She was harassed continually; there were groping hands, lewd suggestions, enforced kisses. This, until Murphy cornered the chief steward with an order, already confirmed with the purser, that stewardesses from the first and second classes were to be detached to accompany Sister Moloney on rounds.

'And not the good-lookers,' Murphy said. 'Battleaxes are what's needed. The nearest to a hospital matron you can find.'

That helped. But there was, as ever, the man who would not be denied and was prepared to wait his opportunity and then take a chance.

At two bells in the afternoon watch, her decks once again clean, the liner took her departure from Funchal. Tom Chatto had laid off a course to take the ship across the South Atlantic for Rio de Janeiro in Brazil, from where they would drop down the South American coast to the River Plate and then the passage of Cape Horn. At their speed of fourteen knots they would be off Rio in ten days' time. And not so long after that, Buenos Aires in the Argentine.

Tom looked forward to the Buenos Aires arrival, when the ship would spend two full days in the port. Tom hoped for shore leave; he had an appointment in Buenos Aires—or he hoped he had: what Bolsover had told him about father Pontarena had given him cause for doubt. But currently the facts were these: Dolores had gone home to the Argentine some months before Tom had left the *Bulolo* and in an exchange of cables before joining the *Orvega* they had made certain arrangements. Tom hoped the girl would be able to keep to them. She had an aunt in Buenos Aires, and this aunt could provide the excuse. But a lot would depend on the aunt. Aunts varied...

Two days out from Funchal in idyllic weather, there was a sea burial to conduct. One of the sick women had died, the first of what was to be many. The dead woman had been accompanied from Liverpool by her five children; no husband—she had been a widow. When the *Orvega* stopped engines and lay still on the blue water of the South Atlantic, the five small orphans—the oldest was nine years of age—made a pathetic group clustered in the after well-deck where their mother's body waited to be lifted to the plank laid over the ship's side in a gap where the guardrail had been removed. Captain Fullbright came down from the bridge to read the simple, poignant committal service.

He glanced at the children; he would have a word with them in the privacy of his cabin after the committal.

There was a heavy silence as the liner lay with her engines stopped, her way off, lying now motionless on the still water, no wind, just a slight roll to the ocean swell. The silence was broken only by the cries of seagulls circling overhead, the inevitable accompaniment of any ship at sea as the daily discharge of galley refuse was awaited.

Fullbright removed his cap, glanced aft to make sure the Red Ensign had been lowered to half-mast, and began the service. As the words of the committal itself were reached, he nodded briefly towards the Chief Officer. The canvas-shrouded body had been lifted by four seamen to the plank; these men now, under Forster's order, began slowly to tilt the plank towards the sea.

'Forasmuch,' Fullbright read, 'as it hath pleased Almighty God of his great mercy to take unto himself the soul of our dear sister here departed, we therefore commit her body to the deep; in sure and certain hope of the Resurrection to eternal life...'

The plank was tilted further. The body slid, dropped towards the sea, lead-weighted at the feet, twisting a little until it vanished beneath the water. It vanished for only a short time; it came back to the surface, rolling and dipping under. Fullbright at once ordered the children to be taken off the well-deck and into the after accommodation: there were things it was better not to see.

'Mr Forster?'

'Sir?'

'Air in the canvas.' Fullbright handed over a single heavy key on a ring. 'My safe key. Be so good as to fetch my revolver.' Forster went off at the double. The passengers began to disperse, urged away from the rails by the Third Officer and the bosun, back to their pleasures. The Chief Officer returned with the Captain's revolver. Fullbright himself went to the guardrail and took aim. A shot kicked up spray around the corpse. The second and third shots found the target; there were bubbles, then slowly the body began to sink. Fullbright, clutching his prayerbook and the revolver incongruously together, turned for'ard and made his way back to the bridge, worrying about the orphaned children. From now on they would be pampered so far as was possible. Fullbright considered getting the purser to berth them in a spare cabin in the second class, but thought better of it: there were going to be more deaths, possibly more orphans, and there were not all that number of spare cabins.

Five minutes later the Chief Engineer on the starting platform below saw the telegraph from the bridge move its pointer to Standby and then to Slow Ahead. Water boiled up beneath the stern and the *Orvega* resumed her course for Rio de Janeiro.

Shortly after Tom Chatto had come off bridge watch that evening, the contact he had been half expecting ever since the Liverpool departure came in the form of a knock on his cabin door by his steward.

'Sorry to bother you, sir.'

'That's all right, Bell. What is it?'

'A message from the purser, sir. A passenger, a man, sir, in the steerage.' Bell spoke disparagingly, indicating that in his view a steerage passenger had no business bothering one of the ship's deck officers. 'The man asks to see you, sir.'

Patience: that was obvious. 'His name?' Tom asked.

'Sivyer, sir.' Bell added, 'He didn't state his business. Purser said, should he give him the brushoff, sir?'

Tom saw no point in that. If Patience wanted to make contact he would make it sooner or later, possibly when Tom was making an inspection of the steerage decks, but clearly he would prefer the privacy of Tom's cabin. 'I'll see him now,' Tom said, bowing to the inevitable; he would make the visit as brief as possible. Bell went off with the message to the purser. Tom's mind raced again over the past. There were those curious elements; the fact that no word had ever come back to the *Pass of Drumochter* as to what had happened to Patience after he had been put aboard the British warship for onward passage to Valparaiso. Valparaiso and justice, probably Chilean justice since the murder of the stowaway had taken place on Chilean territory. There had been total silence; and in fact no one aboard the windjammer had taken pains to inquire: the fact that a brute of a First Mate had been removed from their suffering backs had been good news enough and none had wished him anything but retribution.

Ten minutes after Bell's departure he was back with the so-called Sivyer. The man, cadaverous-looking, with a shake, a sort of uncontrollable tremor, looked to the steward dangerous enough for him to say, 'If you want me, sir—'

'Thank you, Bell, but you needn't worry.'

'If you say so, sir.' Bell, looking doubtful, went on his way. Tom faced the man who was now obviously Patience. It was a curious feeling. The last time they had met Tom had been no more than a first-voyage apprentice, and Patience—*Mister* Patience—the all-powerful First Mate, ship's disciplinarian, hazer and taskmaster, a man to be addressed firmly as 'sir'. Tom couldn't help the feeling of a reversion to the past, a kind of involuntary need to show respect; or at any rate, to watch his step with a senior officer.

Controlling his nerves, he asked, 'What can I do for you, Mr Sivyer?'

'Come off it, boy.' Patience still had traces of the roughneck First Mate. 'No need for that. You know very well who I am. You knew that from the first moment you saw me come aboard.'

'Yes, I did.'

Patience grinned. 'Are you not going to have the courtesy to ask me to sit down, Mr brassbound Second Mate?'

Tom indicated the small cabin's only chair; Patience sat. Tom stood by the bunk. 'Perhaps you'll explain, Mr Patience.'

'They didn't make the charge stick,' Patience said hoarsely. 'The depositions were good enough for the Chileans but it was known that Fontanet, or Chardonnet, was a murderer in the first place. That

63

counted. I got five years in a stinking Chilean gaol. While I was there, I got word from England that my wife had died. No money was going back. She died of sheer bloody neglect and starvation. Got consumption.'

'I'm sorry,' Tom said.

Patience made no comment. He went on, 'When I came out of that hellhole—well, I couldn't get a job back at sea. Not at first. A blank in my discharge book for five years to be explained. No one would look at me. After a while, though, I was signed aboard a rotten, leaking coffin ship as a deckhand. I left her when we docked in Cardiff. At least it got me a passage home. I don't propose to go into details as to how I lived after that. But you may ask, why am I going back to South America? I'll tell you, since it's relevant. I'm going all the way with you, Mr Second Mate, all the way to Valparaiso. I have...unfinished business.'

It was an unsavoury story. Patience was reticent over the details but it seemed that a woman was involved, a Chilean woman in Valparaiso with whom Patience had lived after his release from gaol. This woman would provide him with a home and in time he might find some sort of a job in the town. He would be better able to exist there than in England. In the meantime he needed money. Tom didn't ask how he had been able to provide his passage money: anything was possible—robbery, false pretences—in the dreary descent from grace that had been the ex-First Mate's lot. He could very likely have got out of the country just in time.

But cash was now the nub.

'Luck—luck for me—put you aboard this ship,' Patience said.

'What does that mean?' Tom asked, a cold anger gripping him.

Patience grinned. Adorned by that grin, the face was pure evil. 'It means this: I'm down to my last sixpence. And you're going to rectify my financial position. I'm in need of, let's say, fifty pounds. To you, that's—what?—around five months' pay. To me, it's a new life. What do you say, *Mister* Chatto?'

Tom's face was flushed. 'I say you haven't a snowflake in hell's chance—'

'Yes, I expected that,' Patience said calmly. 'But unless you change your mind, boy, you're going to regret it very much indeed. And don't ask me why. That remains my secret.' Patience got to his feet. 'I'll be in touch again, never fear.'

Worry set in unavoidably. What to do? Go in confidence to the Captain, ask his advice? Tom was reluctant to do that: better to deal with Patience on his own. The events aboard the *Pass of Drumochter*—the stowaway, the murders— were best left in the past rather than raked up before his new company. What could the Captain do anyway, what advice could he give that Tom couldn't think up for himself? There was nothing Patience had done aboard that would justify the Captain in, for instance, putting him ashore in Rio. The conversation with the man in his cabin was a matter of his word against that of Patience. A threat had been uttered, it was true, but there was no proof whatsoever.

What could Patience do against him? Tom racked his brains, looking back into the past, wondering if he had committed some sort of indiscretion, some dereliction of duty aboard the windjammer that Patience could now point a finger to, and get him in the bad books of PSNC. But that was fantasy: no notice would be taken of Patience; and, in any case, Tom's conscience was clear. He had been too much of a new boy in those days for him to have put a foot wrong in any sense derogatory to his character.

Give the man the money, call it a loan? The purser would provide an advance of pay. But fresh demands would come for certain. And to do that would go against the grain, would be an act of moral cowardice.

The worry nagged persistently.

FOUR

Tom Chatto was on bridge watch, looking out in the dawn's light across a smooth sea with only a gentle swell, a sea lying greenish-blue under a multicoloured sky, some 1000 miles out from Madeira, with another 3500 to Rio. No hint of trouble as he paced the bridge in front of the helmsman standing on the raised platform abaft the wheel. No hint until the whine of the engine-room voicepipe broke the dawn's peaceful quiet.

Tom went to the voicepipe, lifted the polished brass cover. 'Bridge,' he said. 'Officer of the Watch—'

The Chief Engineer's urgent voice cut in. 'We'll need to stop engines soonest possible. Low-pressure valve spindle again. Have I permission to stop?'

'I'll call the Captain, Chief. Is this going to be a long job?'

'I can't say yet.' Harrison banged down the voicepipe cover at his end. Deck officers never did understand the problems of engineers. They were never in sympathy with what they liked to call the black gang. Engineers had only fairly recently been accepted as officers, and only second-grade ones at that, and grudgingly. They were segregated in their own mess, not allowed to sully the passenger decks, not, with the sole exception of the Chief himself, permitted a table in the first- or second-class saloons. As the engine-room telegraph clanged and its pointer moved to Stop Engines, Harrison glared ill-temperedly from the starting platform towards his Second Engineer, already preparing to strip down some of the machinery assisted by the junior engineers and the greasers whose job it was to use the long-necked oil injectors that kept the moving parts in a continual state of lubrication. The job was probably going to be a long one. You never could tell until the parts had been laid bare for a full inspection. No one was going to be very pleased, except for the firemen in the boiler rooms. They would get some respite from the continual banking up of the furnaces, though it would not be long enough for the head of steam to be lost, leaving the ship unready to respond when the repair was completed and the bridge demanded way through the water.

Harrison grinned to himself as he left the starting platform to join the Second Engineer. The passengers were certainly not going to be pleased. Passengers never were; and, like sheep, they were inclined to panic when anything happened to disturb the daily routine.

It was, as ever, the purser's staff that would take the brunt of the displeasure. The counter would begin to get crowded once the lack of movement was noted by the passengers awaking to the cups of tea brought by the stewards. It had in fact been the stewards who had been first in line: it was always very obvious aboard a ship when the engine sounds, the vibration and the steady thump of the screws, ceased for any reason.

'What's happened, Steward?'

'Dunno, sir. Captain didn't let on, sir. Just that we've stopped.'

'Well, I know that,' Percival J. Bunce said irritably. He reckoned that he might after all have done better to book his passage in a United States ship. 'What I want to know is why, for Jeez' sake.'

The steward came up with the standard answer: 'Best ask the purser, sir.'

Before breakfast was served, notices were posted around the ship: engines had been stopped for routine repairs following the lack of co-operation from the shore authorities in Funchal. The duration of the stoppage was not yet known but the passengers would be kept informed. Time lost would so far as possible be made up later and it was hoped that the Rio arrival would still be made on time. 'Which,' Harrison remarked to his Second Engineer, 'means that the Old Man's going to want extra knots out of us. I've told him that if he wants that he's maybe asking for more trouble. Deck officers, they're all shellbacks.' In all the liner companies, sail training, the possession of a Master's Certificate in sail, was a cast-iron prerequisite for any officer looking for a berth. But engines, Harrison reflected, didn't operate like the wind. The wind could come and the wind could go, but it didn't suffer mechanical breakdown.

Of all those aboard the *Orvega*, the most immediately worried were the sick in the steerage; and, through them, the doctor and Sister Moloney. The stillness of the ship meant that no fresh air was blowing down from the big bell-mouth ventilators on the boat deck, ventilators that were always turned so as to pick up the wind, being shifted as the wind shifted. There was, as it happened, no wind currently; and because the ship was motionless she was not creating her own wind, as it were, across the decks.

The result was a greatly increased foetidness below, especially in the steerage where there were no ports to be opened to assuage what soon became horrendous conditions.

The influenza had spread alarmingly and had in fact penetrated into both the first- and second-class accommodation. One of

71

those afflicted was the silent Mrs Tidy. Dr Murphy, attending her in her cabin, was worried. The woman was slightly built, almost nothing of her, her limbs thin to the point of emaciation. She had little resistance, vomited up anything she managed to eat. Silent as ever, she didn't complain. Lieutenant Tidy didn't seem worried, however.

'My wife survived India, Doctor. All the epidemics—cholera and so on. A terrible place for sickness, India. We lost nearly half our battalion on the North-West Frontier, lost 'em to the cholera.'

'Your wife didn't get it?'

Tidy shook his head. 'No, nor me as it happened. Picture of health, the two of us.'

'You were younger then,' Murphy pointed out. Now, both husband and wife were in their sixties, going to Buenos Aires to visit their son working in the overseas service of a British insurance company. He hoped the woman would make it. Two hours after the engines had stopped, there was another death, once again in the steerage: a young man going out to find work in the Argentine's meat yards. With the ship stopped indefinitely, there could be no question of an immediate sea burial. Corpses could not be set adrift possibly to remain close to the ship. The body was put into the ship's cold store to await the completion of the repair.

This was not good for morale: the proximity of a body and the ship's provisions was not a happy thought. And there were murmurings coming from the steerage, complaints that the sick were taking second place to the comforts and privileges of the wealthy in the other two classes.

When word of this reached Fullbright from the doctor and the purser he ordered the worst cases to be brought out into the open air of the afterdeck. 'If necessary, we'll use the first- and second-class decks as well,' he said. 'I can well understand those poor devils' feelings.'

The steerage was mollified by this consideration, but only up to a point. The open decks had a limited capacity and many had to be left below to await their turn. And now there were complaints from the other classes. The disease would spread faster—either that or the open decks would have to be boycotted by the gentlemen and their ladies. It wasn't fair, when you thought about the passage money that had been paid in Liverpool.

'It's more serious than I thought, sir.' Harrison, his white overalls crumpled and streaked with oil and grease, had come personally to the bridge when the bugles had blown the passengers to their luncheon. 'We look like being stuck here for a full due... I'm sorry, but there it is. It's not just the valve spindle now. As no doubt you know, sir,' Harrison went on, pretty certain in his own mind that the Old Man didn't know at all, 'the low-pressure valve spindle is important only when manoeuvring in port. Which of course isn't to say that it hadn't to be made serviceable ready for the Rio arrival. It had.'

'Of course, Chief—'

'But now the for'ard spindles on the main engines have fractured.' Harrison took a deep breath. 'Both of them. The luck of the devil! And as yet I can't say how long the job's going to take. But it'll not be quick. We're going to have our work cut out, sir.'

'And meanwhile we can't move.'

'That we can't, no.'

Fullbright glanced across at the Officer

of the Watch standing by the binnacle. 'Mr Chatto, have the purser informed—I'll have notices sent down for the passengers presently.' He glanced up at the foremast: the two black balls indicating the ship not under command, as per Board of Trade regulations in any situation where a ship had lost power, swayed gently in the swell. They would remain there for a while yet. After a sweeping look around the horizons, finding no ship in sight, Fullbright went below to draft informatory notices for the passengers. The delay was going to be longer. That was all. Full information would be passed when more was known.

During the night the wind came. The ship was close to the path of the north-east trades, and a quirk of nature had brought a blow a little more northerly than had been expected. The ship in her stopped position heaved and lurched uneasily and cold wetness swept the bridge and the open decks. The sick had been sent below a little before nightfall; if the bad weather continued, they would have to remain below next day.

As the wind increased, the Third Officer, on watch from midnight to 0400, called the Captain, reporting the wind speed and direction.

'All secure on deck, Mr Parkinson?'

'All secure, sir. The bosun's checked the anchors and cables.'

'All right, Parkinson. Call me at once if there's further increase or any change in direction.'

'Aye, aye, sir.' Parkinson closed the voicepipe cover. He stared ahead through the blackness—the moon was obscured by heavy cloud—and the rain that had now started, driven along by the wind to affect the visibility. He had sent the bridge messenger to the chart room for his oilskin and sou'wester; now he shrugged himself deep into the stiff collar of the oilskin. The cold was a sharp and unwelcome contrast to the day's heat; this was one of the times when a man tended to wish he'd never come to sea. Parkinson knew that before long the wind and rain, and the sea, would increase. Discomfort would increase with it.

Below in the engine room, the work was proceeding round the clock. Harrison himself was there with his staff: it had become a case of All Hands for the black gang, and all of them were weary and dirty with the inevitable engine-room grease. As the *Orvega* began to lurch with the wind-blown sea, men slid on the oily metal deck, reaching out for handholds wherever they could, cursing as their feet went from under them. In the boiler rooms the firemen toiled away, keeping up the reduced steam pressure, looking like devils outlined redly against the glow from the open furnace-mouths. In the cabins, along the close-packed steerage decks, the passengers began to feel the heave and lurch: ships always took a disturbed sea badly when there was no forward motion, when she lay powerless in the ocean's grip. Seasickness, which had been mostly left behind soon after the ship had cleared away from the south of Ireland, took hold again. The result on the steerage decks was a worse stench that pervaded everything.

Patience didn't suffer from seasickness. He lay sleepless, however, listening in disgust to the sounds of the men in his stinking cabin: snores, retching, groans of sheer misery. After a while he could stand it no longer; he got up from the narrow bunk, pulled on a pea jacket and coarse serge trousers, and made his way along the alleyways to the small portion of open deck allocated to the steerage passengers immediately above the rudder and the now motionless screws. The stern heaved, rose and fell to the swell and the roughening sea. Patience glared out into the blackness, felt the force of the wind. Cold and uncomfortable, it was better than the stench; Patience took a deep breath, filling his lungs with fresh air. He still hankered after the sea life, cursed his own folly in having made a return to it impossible, other than in the most menial capacity; cursed young Chatto at the same time. There had been no further contact between them. He felt in his guts that Chatto wasn't going to come up with any cash, knew, too, that his own threat had been in reality an empty one. He had nothing he could use against Chatto. Not yet, anyway. But he would be watching out for an opportunity. Cash he had to have. Somehow or other, he would get it.

By now Fullbright was on the bridge: the blow had worsened quite suddenly at the time of the change of watch. Tom, taking over at 0400 for the morning watch, had felt the sudden drop in pressure, the warning sign of gale force winds to come. He had called the Captain, alerted the bosun who had called out the hands to recheck all the falls and griping bands of the lifeboats and put extra wire strops on the anchor cables to back up the Blake slips and bottle-screw slips on the fo'csle-head. The funnel stays were checked and tautened where necessary; and a warning went to the engine room that worse weather was on the way.

Tom asked, 'How's it going, Chief? Any forecast as to when you'll be—'

Fullbright had taken over the voicepipe when Harrison answered, his temper badly frayed by this time: 'That's the sort of daft question I'd expect from the bridge. Bloody fools the lot of you, ought to get your bloody heads read—'

Fullbright grinned: he understood the black gang better than Harrison would give him credit for, and he sympathized with their difficulties when under pressure from the bridge, and ultimately from the Owners as well. He said, 'There's nothing like honesty, Chief, is there?'

There was an exclamation from far below. 'I'm sorry, sir—'

'That's all right. I know you're doing

your best. I'll ask no more questions.'

Fullbright put back the cover. As he did so, the full force of the gale struck. The *Orvega* gave a heavy lurch; the wind made a sound like a devil's orchestra as it howled through the standing rigging, round the masts and yards, twanging at the funnel stays, lifting the canvas covers of the lifeboats; the rain came down in heavy sheets that took away the remains of the visibility, soaked through the oilskins of the men on the open bridge.

In the after part of the ship, Patience felt the sudden change, was virtually blown along the decks and through the door into the steerage alleyway. Making his way along, staggering to the lift and fall of the deck, reaching out his arms to act as fenders to keep him off the bulkheads to either side, he came upon a figure, a woman, collapsed on the deck outside one of the female lavatories.

He bent; the woman was unconscious. There was blood coming from a gash on her head; she had, he guessed, slipped on the vomit-slimed deck and struck her head on a projection of the bulkhead. Patience had a sudden thought. Quickly he looked around, up and down the alleyway. There was no one else about. He acted quickly. He bent again to the unconscious woman, a middle-aged woman, pale and scrawny, whom he'd seen from time to time on deck, a woman with a consumptive look. He rummaged through the thin, cheap clothing, pulled up the dress. He found what he was looking for: a body belt beneath the underclothing. In the belt's pouch he felt the presence of coins. He opened the buttoned flap. Two gold sovereigns glittered in the faint glow from the police lights on the deckhead above. These he pocketed quickly, then straightened the woman's clothing. Within two minutes he was back in his cabin. A little later the woman was found by a prowling nightwatchman of the master-at-arm's staff. This man went for the doctor; the woman was removed to the surgery. In the morning she died. When this news reached Patience, he was relieved. There would be no report of missing money. And after all, she wouldn't be needing those two sovereigns now. But it was a nasty thought, when it penetrated the many layers of degradation with which Patience had covered himself during the mean years: he had virtually robbed a corpse.

'*Look out aft, there!*' It was Tom who had yelled into the wind. Fullbright looked up, looked astern. He saw the falling yard, ducked as it flew over the bridge, smashing into the side of the chart room on its way. Glass shattered, woodwork splintered. The bridge was a mess. No one had been hurt, but it was something of a miracle that they hadn't been. The heavy maintopmast yard, carried clear from its parral, had torn away one of the funnel stays on its path to the bridge. And not content with smashing in the chart-room bulkhead, its great length had sent its arm smashing into the wheel itself. Until a repair could be effected, the ship would be forced to steer by use of the emergency steering position aft once the engine room was in action again.

Tom sent down for the carpenter. The man was sanguine: a repair could be made but it wouldn't be a quick job. In the meantime the chart room stood open to wind and sea, the sea that was now flinging spray as high as the bridge itself. The carpenter went below to fetch up canvas that would be used as dodgers pending repair.

As a wet and dreary forenoon came

up, the watches were changed as usual but the ship's officers, apart from the purser and his first assistant, did not attend breakfast in the saloon. They were required elsewhere until the gale abated. At the purser's table there were many empty seats, the weather having taken its toll of appetites. One of those present was a Mrs Handley, travelling to Valparaiso on what she referred to, somewhat mysteriously, as 'business', seeming reluctant to elaborate. Purser Ainsworth knew she was a married woman but unaccompanied by her husband who, she said, was a civil servant bound by the chains of duty to Whitehall. Mrs Handley was an attractive woman, aged about thirty-two. Ainsworth's long experience of life aboard the liners had taught him that attractive women in their thirties, travelling without their husbands, could pose certain problems for ship's officers. And various probing remarks from the lady earlier in the voyage had pointed Ainsworth's attention in a very definite direction.

'The young man with two stripes, Mr Ainsworth,' she'd said, lightly enough. 'Who is he?'

'I think you mean the Second Officer.'

'I expect I do. *So* good-looking. Do tell me his name, won't you?'

Ainsworth had done so. Mrs Handley had nodded, with a look in her hazel eyes which said that she was going to be an example of that particular problem that Ainsworth had encountered so many times. Foreign shores, foreign waters, blue seas, indigo seas at night beneath the moon, brassbound uniforms and the glamour that always went with the sea and those who sailed upon it so adventurously, did uneasy things to a woman on her own who was missing the comforts of married life. There was something about a ship at sea that loosened morals; the officers and passengers were in a kind of limbo, in a world apart, a world divorced from normal, everyday life; what went on aboard ship took place in a cocoon and would never, or need never, be known to those ashore. But ships' officers had nevertheless to watch their step: cabin-crawling was not popular with the Owners. Their liners had a reputation to preserve. The signals could be set for danger. Ainsworth tinkered with the idea of a word of warning, but decided to refrain. Tom Chatto, though relatively inexperienced in the ways of liners, should be able to look after himself without a nanny in the background.

This morning Mrs Handley, bright and cheerful despite the weather, had noted the absence of the Second Officer.

'No Mr Chatto. I suppose he's busy on the bridge. Or somewhere. The forenoon's not his watch, is it?'

'No,' Ainsworth said. Mrs Handley-Grace Handley as she had told him although he knew this already from the passenger lists—had done some homework. 'The gale, you know. Makes work for the deck department.'

'Such a shame.' Mrs Handley gave Ainsworth a covert look, faintly coquettish. Possibly any man would do, but she was unlikely to set her cap at an ageing purser. Ainsworth was well on the wrong side of fifty, with a wife and three children in Liverpool, and knew he looked much married. Also, he had a paunch. One lived well in the liners of PSNC, and gin helped to put on fat. Romance was aimed strictly at the younger deck officers. Ainsworth didn't mind; he was too close to his pension to take any risks. He steered the conversation away from possible or indeed probable shipboard affairs, switching it to the Rio arrival. They looked like being adrift on their ETA, he said.

'ETA?'

'Estimated Time of Arrival, Mrs Handley.'

'Oh dear. Can't the Captain do something about it?'

Ainsworth smiled rather bleakly. Passengers were all the same, basically. He said, 'The Captain does what he can. This time it's in the hands of the Chief Engineer.'

Mrs Handley giggled girlishly. 'And God.'

'God?'

'He rules the waves.'

'Oh—yes, of course, certainly. But it's not really the waves, it's the—'

'The bloody engine. Oh, please don't look shocked, Mr Ainsworth. I'm only repeating what I heard the head waiter say.'

Maybe, Ainsworth thought, but a lady shouldn't repeat what head waiters said. If his own wife or daughters had used the word he would have thought the end of the world had come.

The gale continued; the mess on the bridge was cleared up but until the weather moderated nothing would be done about the chart room: the concentration was on the repairs to the vital ship's steering. Likewise the maintopmast yard would not be replaced in current conditions. That fact pointed up to Tom one of the differences between sail and steam. In sail, you had to disregard the weather; it would be vital to replace any smashed yard as soon as possible, and the hands had to accept the risk of being blown overboard, or smashed to a pulp on the deck so far below, if wind and sea threw them from their always precarious hold upon the foot ropes. In a steamship, you could afford to wait; the yards were not all that important.

During that afternoon, Mrs Tidy gave up her fragile ghost and died: one more body for the cold store. Fortunately, apart from the woman who had provided Patience with funds, no one else died. It began to seem as though the influenza was working its way out: no further cases were reported. Dr Murphy took a half-hour off to entertain Sister Moloney in his cabin: a small gin and bitters each.

'Nice to be out of the stench,' Murphy said, referring to the steerage. 'I don't know how they stand it.'

'Some,' Anne Moloney said, 'stand it better than others.'

Murphy raised an eyebrow. 'Meaning?'

'Some accept, some complain—'

'Isn't that always the way?'

'Yes, it is. But...oh, I don't know, Doctor.' Anne was dead tired and showed it; the hand holding the gin glass had something of a shake. 'There's a bunch of them, ones who haven't gone down with the flu. They've made it plain they find the sick nothing but a nuisance, won't help out, make nasty remarks about the so-called toffs in the first and second class. They seem out to make trouble. Haven't you noticed it?'

'I can't say I have, no. But you can't blame them, perhaps. The differences are pretty glaring, after all—'

'So they are ashore, in everyday life. It's nothing out of the ordinary.' Anne seemed to go off at a tangent. 'I came across one of the men this morning...somehow or other he'd wandered into the first class. I recognized him as one of the...hard cases, I suppose you might call them. I told him to get out. He was quite abusive. Luckily the master-at-arms happened to come along and heard him. He got the man's name. Sivyer, it sounded like.' Anne grinned. 'He didn't argue with the master-at-arms. Well, he did, but he was soon shouted down.'

'That's rather what I was saying,' Murphy said. 'The master-at-arms wouldn't shout at first- or second-class passengers.' He didn't pay much attention to what Anne Moloney had said, but he was to find the incident coming back to him later in the voyage.

Patience was seething. He'd found it easy enough to hop over the locked-gate barriers between the ship's three classes but he hadn't expected to be bowled out so soon. He had things to do in the first class, things to find out, if he could, about Mister Chatto. He had no clear idea what, but reconnaissance was always a help.

He'd been confronted by that bossy nurse, all starch and veil, cuffs and a sharp voice. Young and pretty, which in a way had made it worse. Years before, as First Mate of a windjammer, he'd been (or had thought he was) an attraction to the young ladies in the ports of call on the South American run and in the many saloons along the Australian coast.

'I've seen you before,' the girl said,

starch in her voice to match the uniform.

'Well, good on yer,' Patience had said in a fake Australian accent.

'In the steerage. Will you kindly leave the first-class decks at once?'

'Just because you say so? Not bloody likely!'

'Very well. Then I'll call the master-at-arms.'

Patience jeered. 'How? Blow a whistle? Yell rape? Stupid bitch!'

That was when the master-at-arms had appeared out of a side alleyway. The master-at-arms had put on Patience's arm the sort of grip he'd put on the arms of ratings returning aboard his battleship the worse for drink. Master-at-Arms Brasher had been just about the toughest disciplinarian the ship's company of the *Lord Nelson* had ever known. Patience didn't protest for very long.

But he would be back. Chatto was to get his comeuppance if it was to be over Patience's dead body.

Fullbright was in his day cabin when the voicepipe gave a whistle.

'Captain speaking...'

'Chief Engineer, sir. Repair's completed,

at any rate jury-rig fashion. We'll need dockyard assistance for a full job. Will I turn the engines over for a test run?'

'Do that, Chief—and thank you.' Fullbright put back the voicepipe cover and went fast for the bridge ladder. 'Telegraphs to stand by,' he ordered. Then, when the repeat had come from the starting platform, he ordered the engines to Slow Ahead. He waited for a response from the Chief Engineer. When Harrison reported all well, Fullbright said, 'I'll put the telegraphs to Half Ahead, Chief. Build up the revolutions as you think fit, then if all goes well we'll go at once to full away.'

Within the next few minutes the *Orvega* began once again to move through the water, dead slow at first, then faster as Harrison watched his bearings, his dials and gauges, nursing his noisy kingdom back to life. A half-hour later, with the ship being steered from the after-steering position pending the restoration of the main steering, the liner was moving fast ahead and the ventilators turned to catch the wind, which was still blowing at full force. There was relief in all classes as the terrible humid stuffiness was blown away.

FIVE

As the ship dropped south-westerly towards Brazil, and finally left the north-east trade winds behind her, the weather became completely different. The sun shone from a clear blue sky whose colour was reflected in the sea; the ship's wake left a white kurfuffle behind her as she steamed at full speed now to make up time lost. The cold store was cleared of bodies and the delayed sea burials took place, the Captain once again officiating as the engines were briefly stopped. On Sunday Fullbright acted in another parsonic capacity, taking Divine Service in the first-class lounge, crammed for the occasion with such of the other classes as wished to attend and could find room. God was a democrat, after all, everyone equal in His sight, even the steerage passengers. Tom Chatto, off watch and attending the service, was reminded of his military brother and of visits to his regiment at the Curragh: normally it had been a case of officers and their ladies, sergeants and their wives, the men and their women. But at church parade it hadn't applied with quite the same force.

Deck games were started: quoits. Tom had become fairly proficient at quoits during his time in the Royal Mail liners. He was congratulated by Grace Handley, who clapped rather obviously whenever he landed his quoit successfully.

'Oh, well done, Mr Chatto,' she said when a game ended. She was sitting in a deck chair; she patted the one next to her.

'I've been keeping it for you,' she said, smiling up at him. She removed a book and her handbag. 'Do sit down and talk to me.'

'That's very kind of you, Mrs Handley,' Tom said. He was about to sit when he became aware of a certain frigidity behind him. He turned, and was faced by a passenger who had been favoured with the Captain's table in the first-class saloon: Lady Moyra Bentinck, daughter of an earl, widow of a major general. The look in Lady Moyra's eye was enough. Ships' officers did not take up chairs when they were required by passengers. There were others available but Lady Moyra

93

wanted this one: she wished to talk to Mrs Handley. Tom gave a slight bow of apology and moved away. He caught Mrs Handley's eye: daggers were there, daggers for Lady Moyra as a vast bulk settled itself alongside her.

Lady Moyra started the conversation. 'So nice to have fine weather, don't you think?'

'Lovely.'

'So sad about the deaths. Those poor children.'

'Yes.'

'I've been thinking...really, a collection should be started. They're probably penniless, don't you know. Quite penniless. I thought I might mention it to the Captain at luncheon.'

'What a good idea.'

'Yes, well.' Lady Moyra was somewhat irritated by the woman's taciturnity. It was rude, to a person in her position, not to be more forthcoming, more enthusiastic. Children were children, poor little mites, and a good cause was a good cause. It was up to the more fortunate to do good. But of course the woman was really rather common. Lady Moyra, given to finding things out, had found out that the absent Mr Handley was a civil servant. She had not found out which department of state enjoyed his services. There were civil servants and civil servants; there was the Foreign Office, there was the India Office; there were also the others. The Home Office was acceptable, just, as was the Treasury. But then there were the lesser ones, and of course there were grades: administrative, executive, clerical, but naturally one didn't concern oneself with the clerical. Lady Moyra rather fancied that Mr Handley would be executive, thus not out of the top drawer; but you never could tell. Lady Moyra, heaving her bosom towards Grace Handley, started off on a different tack. She would work around to Mr Handley later.

'That young man.'

'Who?'

'The one who almost took my chair.'

'It wasn't your chair. I had my book and my handbag on it.'

'I—see.' Lady Moyra gave a sound of annoyance. 'Then I apologize, of course. But ship's sailors shouldn't...well, never mind. I was going on to say that Captain Fullbright was talking about him last night.

At dinner, don't you know. Mr Chatto, I believe he is.'

'Yes.'

'A good family. The father's a dean.' Deans were All Right; almost Foreign Office in a sense. 'A brother in the army, the Connaught Rangers, a good regiment. I've heard my husband say so. Captain Fullbright seemed to think he had a good future in front of him, though whether or not one would call the Merchant Service a good future I really don't know, don't you know.'

'I imagine,' Grace Handley said sweetly, 'it's what he wanted to do.'

'Yes, I suppose so. Yes.'

'What else do you know about him, Lady Bentinck?'

'Lady *Moyra.*' There was an annoyed click of teeth. Really, the sheer *ignorance* of some people. 'I really know nothing else about him, Mrs Handley, nothing beyond what Captain Fullbright said. But,' she added with a touch of venom, 'I do think that a young man's future, whatever it is, is—is important. Not to be in any way compromised.'

She levered herself to her feet. 'You must excuse me, Mrs Handley. I find fresh air rather tiring.' She moved heavily away along the deck, reaching for a guardrail as the deck lifted to the South Atlantic swell. It was true she didn't know any more about the young man than Captain Fullbright had told her; but there had been other things, not revealed to Mrs Handley, that Captain Fullbright had said—said jovially, it was true, not in any way critically: Lady Moyra knew very well, from what she had seen of Captain Fullbright, that he would never criticize his officers to a third party. Captain Fullbright had indeed spoken only in a general sense about young officers and their susceptibilities afloat, and he'd laughed about it while at the same time saying seriously enough that shipboard dalliance could affect careers. And Lady Moyra, accustomed, until her husband had achieved staff rank, to a lifetime of regimental interference in the affairs of others, had taken to watching Mrs Handley and knew her for precisely what she was. And, just now, she had seen that Mrs Handley had taken the intended hint. And also that she had taken umbrage.

Lieutenant and Quartermaster Tidy had been totally shocked by his wife's unexpected death. He had been convinced, as he had told Dr Murphy, of her powers of endurance. India, and all that. He had watched her body sink, not really believing what he was seeing. He had spent the remainder of that terrible day in his cabin, refusing the meals that his steward had offered to bring so that he could avoid having to talk to people at table in the saloon. He had been devastated. Their son in the Argentine had been informed by cable from the ship's wireless office; so far there had been no response. Tidy longed for some sort of communication from his son.

Next day, when the bar opened, Tidy began to take seriously to drink. Brandy was the best way, the quickest.

'Poor old bugger,' the bar steward remarked later that day to the chief bar-keeper. 'All the signs are there, four large ones inside an hour. Can't really blame him, can you, eh? He was probably a bit of a boozer in the Army an' all...'

At dinner that night, Tom noticed that Tidy was missing. The reason appeared to be known to Bolsover, the returning *estancia* manager. 'Boozed,' he said briefly.

The stringy Mrs Tomkin, bank manager's wife, looked scandalized. Bolsover, who had also had quite a lot to drink, possibly helping out Tidy with his sorrows, belched and said, 'No need to wear that prim expression, Mrs Tomkin. Enough to turn the bloody milk sour you are.'

The bank manager leaned across the table. 'Kindly do not speak to my wife like that, Mr Bolsover.'

'Oh, nuts.'

Tomkin bridled. 'Really! I demand an apology. Here and now, or we leave the table.'

'Bugger off if you want, it's no skin off my nose.'

Angrily, muttering to themselves, the Tomkins left. Tom did his best to engage the others in conversation. It was his job to keep his table happy, ensure that they all enjoyed their voyage with PSNC. It was the hardest part of going to sea.

'I overheard the contretemps,' Grace Handley said after dinner, encountering—by design—Tom on the starboard side of the boat deck. 'What a couple! The Tomkins. Typical bank manager. I'm so sorry for that poor man. The soldier.' Then she giggled. 'How *do* you cope, for heaven's sake?'

'With my table? I don't really. I just keep them talking. Mostly about themselves.'

'I suppose that's the secret.' She paused, looking up into his eyes. There happened to be a bright moon, its light falling across the griped-in lifeboats and leaving pools of darkness in their lee. 'Tell me, Mr Chatto—Tom, if I may?' She didn't wait for an answer. 'Do you ever talk about yourself?'

He was embarrassed. 'Well—no. Not unless someone asks.'

'I'm asking now.'

He shrugged. He told her something about his days in the windjammers and she was impressed. He said it was nothing unusual, that all deck officers aspiring to command in steam had to do their time in sail first. He told her of the west of Ireland, of the tame life of the deanery. She listened to it all, and he felt her hand slide into his. She started talking about herself, of her life in London. Dull, she said. Her husband hadn't much money and had seemed to have missed out as regards promotion, being unlikely to go further at his age—fifty-six, a lot older than herself. They lived in Fulham, no great shakes. Her husband was a dry stick, keen on bowls, playing with a lot of other dry old sticks and their ghastly wives.

'It's been a pretty foul life one way and another. It should be better in South America. I've got a sister there, a secretary in Valparaiso. She works for some sort of magnate, a man in minerals, would you believe it—copper ore, iron ore, nitrates, that sort of thing. Terribly boring. But Joanna, that's my sister, she may be able to get me fitted in somewhere. I've done a course in typewriting and general secretarial work. I just hope I'll like it out there, and settle.'

'And your husband?' Tom asked.

'He may come out later, I don't know. He'll retire in just under four years.' Tom felt his hand squeezed and she moved closer. He was, had been for some time, aware of her scent, which was a seductive one. Although older than himself, she attracted him. She seemed defenceless, obviously not in tune with her husband, the dry bowls-playing stick. But Tom was cautious: he needed no one to point out the dangers of a shipboard involvement and he was unsure if he wished to become involved in any case. Awkwardly he said, 'You'll be lonely, Mrs Handley.'

'Grace.' He realized, too late, that he'd made a bloomer. She said, 'Be nice to me, Tom.'

He had been suddenly scared. He was a normal young man; but those dangers loomed: passengers were not allowed to be entertained in officers' cabins, officers were not allowed to enter passengers' cabins. It could be done clandestinely, but at great risk. There were so many prying eyes. He excused himself, murmuring something about his morning watch and the need to turn in for some sleep first. She let him go immediately: he saw that he had hurt her, that she found him guilty of a small act of cowardice. She remained by the lifeboat as he walked for'ard along the boat deck. At the door leading to the main staircase giving access to the first-class accommodation, a bulky figure loomed, one that Tom recognized: the VIP passenger, widow of a major general who had been Chief of Staff to Sir Redvers Buller in the South African war. Lady Moyra Bentinck had clearly seen his emergence from the lifeboat's lee.

'Good evening, Mr Chatto,' she said.

'Good evening, Lady Moyra.' She was obviously expecting him to pause. He did. She went on, 'I understand from Captain Fullbright that you've a brother in the Connaught Rangers?'

'Yes, I have. He's at the Curragh.'

She nodded. 'Such a pleasant station, although the Irish can be troublesome. The Catholic ones, don't you know. I understand you're Church of Ireland, a Protestant, of course.'

Tom sensed that she was filling in, waiting for something to happen. A moment later it did: Grace Handley emerged from the shadows, straight into the moon's light. Lady Moyra had now finished with Tom. 'Good night, Mr Chatto,' she said abruptly.

Not looking back at Grace Handley, Tom went to his cabin below the bridge. Up to a point it had been a lucky escape; to have walked for'ard in company with Grace Handley would have provided the old harridan with more positive ammunition. And there was another thought: the grapevine, the galley wireless, had already told him that Patience, or Sivyer, had been bowled out by Sister Moloney and the master-at-arms in the first-class accommodation. Patience would obviously have been there for a purpose. If the galley wireless should ever alert Patience to any cabin-visiting on Tom's part, that would give the man his lever.

That could not be risked on any account.

There was another thought, one that Tom knew should have occurred to him earlier: Dolores Pontarena would, with any luck, meet him in Buenos Aires. He looked forward to that meeting. Any disloyalty between now and Buenos Aires would have its effect on his conscience. Disloyalty was perhaps not the word: Tom was unsure of the depths of his feeling for Dolores. It was now some while since they had last met in the Far East; both of them could have changed. Marriage, an engagement even, had not been formally spoken of. Yet Tom was undoubtedly rather more than fond of the girl and also he would like to meet her family and see her home background. To have had an affair in the meantime, even just a shipboard one, would go against the grain of Tom's basic honesty. Further, he had the feeling that Grace Handley, given any encouragement, would cling.

With no more trouble in the engine room, the *Orvega* made her landfall for Rio de Janeiro, lay off to await the pilot, then proceeded inwards to one of the world's most beautiful bays. Passing through the entry channel, only some three-quarters of a mile across from land to land, the *Orvega* steamed into a waterway fifteen miles across at its head. To the west of the entry stood Pão de Azúcar, or the Sugar Loaf, a great conical hill 1250 feet in height. The bay itself was dotted with many islands, the largest of which, the Ilha do Governador, six miles long and two miles across, contained the offices of the port authority. On the north side of Ilha das Cobras, and on Mucangue Pequena, there were extensive and largely newly-constructed docks and a coal depot where the ship would once again take bunkers. As the liner came alongside her berth, the various officials boarded and pratique was granted without the difficulties encountered at Funchal. The Chief Engineer went ashore to make personal representations about his engine repair. Stores came alongside in horse-drawn vehicles and were hoisted inboard by the ship's derricks under the supervision of the First Officer and the bosun, with the second steward checking quantities against a list. A batch of Admiralty Notices to Mariners came aboard with the agent and Tom was kept busy with the necessary corrections to his charts. After a couple of hours the Chief Engineer returned aboard and was closeted with the Captain for some while. As Tom worked on the charts, Fullbright came into the chart room.

'News,' he said. 'There'll be some who'll like it but I'm damned if I do myself. The shore people are going to need us here for the best part of a week and the Owners aren't going to be pleased. What about you, Mr Chatto?'

'Me, sir?'

'Yes, you, sir, who the devil else am I speaking to? Been in Rio before, have you?'

'No, sir. The Porter Holt ships—'

'Used Recife—yes, of course. Well, young man, watch your step when you go ashore, that's my advice. Though I suppose the locals are much the same as in any other South American port. They'll all have the shirt off your back, given the chance. And watch out for the women.' Fullbright laughed. 'If I'm teaching my grandmother, just say so, I don't mind.'

Before Tom could respond, Purser Ainsworth loomed in the doorway. 'If you have a moment, sir—'

'Go ahead, Purser. What is it now?'

'Trouble, I'm afraid, sir. Mr Tidy, first-class passenger. A complaint from Lady Moyra Bentinck—'

'Oh, my God, not her! The Owners think the sun shines out of her backside. What's Tidy done, raped her?'

Ainsworth smiled. 'Not as bad as that, sir. Or not quite as bad. He fell over her. The worse for drink, he was. Lady Moyra's sprained her ankle—she fell over with him, in the first-class lounge.'

Fullbright sighed. 'The doctor?'

'Yes, he's seen to her, sir. She's not badly damaged, but she'll have to rest. And she's going to make trouble. She says Mr Tidy should be locked up or put ashore in Rio.'

'She would. Can't you pacify her?'

Ainsworth, keeping a straight face, said, 'She prefers to be pacified by you, sir.'

'That sounds ominous. Oh, very well,

I'll see her just as soon as she's on her feet again.'

Ainsworth said, 'I don't think that'll do, sir. She wants you to go to her stateroom. If I may suggest...I think the sooner the better.'

Fullbright glanced up at the clock on the chart-room bulkhead. He blew out his cheeks in exasperation. 'All right, Purser. Tell her—with my compliments—I'll be down in half an hour.' He added, 'I think I'll have a chaperone.'

'Her maid'll be there, sir—'

'I mean a *ship's* chaperone, someone on my side. Not the stewardess, either. How are you placed, Ainsworth?'

'I'll be there, sir.'

Fullbright nodded his thanks. 'What about Tidy?'

'Taken care of, sir. Put to bed in his cabin. His steward'll keep watch.'

'Right. I'd better see him some time, too. I'll let you know.'

Ainsworth left the chart room. Tom carried on with his corrections, inking in the memoranda in red where they affected the ship's track to Valparaiso and back eventually to Liverpool. He pondered on Lady Moyra: the woman seemed to be a fire-eater. He hoped she wasn't going to pursue the emergence of Grace Handley from those boat-deck shadows earlier. Not that she could make much of that, surely. But any gossip brought to the Captain's attention was to be taken seriously.

Lieutenant and Quartermaster Tidy, ex-regimental quarter-master sergeant in the Lincolnshire Regiment, thence given a quartermaster's non-combatant commission in the Loyal North Lancashires, had served in South Africa. His ultimate commander had been Sir Redvers Buller. He had known of Major General Francis Bentinck, albeit distantly. He had been with the columns that had marched north from Cape Town to the Modder River. Lady Moyra had not, of course, been with those columns, but had gone by sea to Durban to await the arrival of her husband in Natal. And there had been talk, talk that had penetrated down to RQMS Tidy: Lady Moyra, slimmer then than she was now, and some eight years younger, was said on good authority (the Lincolnshire's regimental sergeant major had overheard the adjutant talking to the colonel on the field telephone) to have been engaged in a liaison with a brigadier general, also on Buller's staff but sent ahead to Durban on preparations for Buller's shift of HQ to that city once he had dealt (as subsequently he did not) with the Boer farmers.

Tidy, boozed though he currently was, intended to remember that. And to make good use of it. He knew that Lady Moyra was going to make trouble, and that the Captain was bound to mollify her with some sort of retribution against himself. One sanction would probably be to cut off his alcohol supply, forbid him the ship's bars, and that Tidy could not contemplate.

He pulled on jacket and trousers and emerged unsteadily from his cabin. Outside, he looked up and down the alleyway: no sign of his steward. He proceeded unmolested to the boat deck. Lady Moyra's stateroom would be up there somewhere, where the nobs lived in greater luxury than the ordinary first class. A suite it would be, really, complete with bathroom and maid's berth. Very nice for some, and Lady Moyra—God knew he hadn't *meant* to fall over the old bitch—wasn't going to like being shown up before her classy mates as someone who'd had it off with a brother officer of her husband's.

Mr Tidy's timing was unfortunate: he reached Lady Moyra's stateroom door at the same moment as the Captain and the purser. Under the gaze of the two officers, Mr Tidy lurched to an unsteady halt. The purser spoke first. 'Mr Tidy, sir,' he said to Fullbright.

Tidy gave the Captain no chance to respond. He uttered a loud belch, brandy-filled. Fullbright took a pace backward. Tidy said, 'I'd not go in there if I was you, Captain. It's likely a whorehouse. Because that's what she is, a bloody whore...'

It had been one of the most difficult passenger encounters that Fullbright had known in some thirty years at sea. The purser had done his best to cut off further speech from Tidy but a good deal of explicit information had emerged in a torrent of anger before Tidy had been led away. The racket had brought stewards to the scene and the master-at-arms had attended to escort the ex-soldier back to his cabin. Before his enforced departure, Lady

Moyra had hobbled from her stateroom. She had heard more of the tirade before the master-at-arms had clamped a hammy hand over Tidy's mouth. 'That,' she said, 'is the drunken person who fell over me. What is he shouting about?'

'Lady Moyra—'

'Will you kindly answer my question, Captain Fullbright?'

Tidy managed to bite the master-at-arm's hand. 'Fornicating bitch,' he said loudly in the moment that the hand was withdrawn.

'Lady Moyra, if you'd be so good as to go back to your cabin.' Fullbright placed a hand firmly on her shoulder and swung her round, wishing he could plant a foot on her backside to speed the process. Lady Moyra, however, seemed to recognize the authority behind the hand on her shoulder. She submitted. Once inside the stateroom she collapsed on to her bed. 'That appalling man,' she said, sniffing. A hint of tears now, and her face was a mess. 'Perhaps you can explain, Captain Fullbright.'

Fullbright took a deep breath. 'I'll do my best,' he said. He wondered just how much the woman had overheard.

SIX

Next day Tom changed out of uniform and went ashore. From the promenade deck Grace Handley watched him go down the gangway. A few moments later she followed. She caught up with Tom.

'Good morning, Mr Chatto.'

Tom raised his hat. 'Good morning, Mrs Handley.'

She giggled. 'We can stop being formal now, can't we?'

'Is this wise?' he asked, and she gave a peal of laughter.

'Don't be such a goody-goody! The old trout's sting has been well and truly drawn. Or haven't you heard?'

'Yes,' he said. 'I've heard.' The whole ship had heard; the galley wireless had had a field day, and this time there was no question of its being only rumour. The fracas had been too loud for that, thanks to Tidy. Tidy had been given the punishment he had feared. Fullbright had sent him to his quarters and given him a dressing-down such as would in Tidy's army days have been accorded a defaulting recruit. Tidy was to be allowed no more drink; and if he repeated his behaviour, if he uttered one more word derogatory to Lady Moyra Bentinck, then he risked being placed under restraint in his cabin and being landed at Rio before the liner sailed for Buenos Aires.

For Lady Moyra herself, the result had been totally devastating. Whore, fornicator, stuffed by a brass hat serving under her husband, bitch, hussy, loose woman, and whore again. The whole ship knew about it. Whether or not it was true was not the point. Lady Moyra's reputation had gone for a burton and it was unlikely she would emerge from her stateroom before she disembarked at Valparaiso.

'So that's that,' Grace Handley said. She took Tom's arm. '*She* won't gossip now.'

'She's not the only one aboard.'

'Oh,' Grace said, 'don't *spoil* things, Tom love!'

Love. Tom thought: Oh well, what the hell, Uncle Benjamin, to the Dean's disgust and fury, had once spoken of a woman in every port. And come to that, Tom in his years at sea hadn't led a totally blameless life. You were young only once, he reminded himself now. A cliché, maybe, but true enough. What nagged was Dolores Pontarena and the forthcoming rendezvous in Buenos Aires.

They went sightseeing. Rio was a fine city and a romantic one, with splendid beaches and luxurious hotels—a playground of the very rich. But a seamy side existed close by in the poverty and squalor of the overcrowded backstreets and alleys. They lunched in a hotel on the waterfront, a meal that cost Tom rather more than a month's pay. This was after they had wandered round the city, which had stood since 1567 on the west side of the bay. They looked at the Cattete Palace, residence of the President of the republic, and the Palacete Itamaraty, official residence of the Minister for Foreign Affairs, at the great government printing office, one of the finest of the city's edifices. Botanical gardens, splendid parks...the cathedral, the medical school, the polytechnic, the national library and the observatory on Morro do Castello, not to mention the military and naval academies and the arsenal, would have to be left until another run ashore if Tom could get leave. That afternoon, Grace wanted to see something away from the wealth and splendour: the other face of Rio. Slumming, she said, was always fun. And while the waterfront hotels and the civic buildings made one feel poor by comparison, the hovels in the poor quarters would give one a self-indulgent but satisfactory sense of wealth.

She was insistent; and Tom went along with her wish. You might as well see everything when you had the chance, although personally he had no desire to gloat. His time in sail had been hard enough, the conditions of the fo'c'sle hands even harder. That had given Tom an immense sympathy with the underdog.

The seamy side of Rio was, he found, little different from the equivalent parts of Valparaiso or other South American ports. There was the same smell from the open drains, the same attentions from the flies clustering on the dungheaps, the same ragged, shoeless children begging in the alleys, the same semi-naked women eyeing the strangers from the doorways of their hovels. They both found that before long they had had enough. They made their way back to more salubrious streets.

Before they had left the alleys they also found Patience.

Patience had gone ashore to enjoy his stolen sovereigns. He had in fact gone ashore to find a woman. Women were not hard to find in the swarming alleys. Patience was choosy, however. He didn't take the first offering from the small boy who, like the small boys of Port Said, offered his sister's services. The services were cheap; too cheap. Patience eventually selected a dusky, well-breasted girl of perhaps seventeen, having prudently changed his golden sovereigns into small units of Brazilian currency. He was leaving the girl's premises—a raised earthen bed covered with a flea-ridden rug in a room shared with some chickens, a mangy dog, and an old woman asleep in one corner—when he saw Tom coming along the alley. With a woman. Patience hadn't seen the woman before, but made the obvious deduction that she was a passenger from the *Orvega*.

He stepped out in front of the couple.

'Well, if it isn't *Mister* Chatto. You'll introduce me to the lady, no doubt?'

Tom flushed, caught off guard. Patience

was a passenger, even if a steerage one. But Tom was not going to make overtures to any man who had uttered threats, tried to extort money. He said, 'I'm sorry. I'm due back aboard...no time to stop.'

He walked on. Grace kept pace with him but looked back. Patience shouted after them, 'Hoity-toity, eh! Stuck up little prig with a fancy tart. But I'll get even, just you mark my words.'

'Who's that?' Grace asked, quickening her pace.

No point in going into details. Not yet, anyway. Tom said, 'A steerage passenger. One to keep clear of. Dangerous—like Lady Moyra.'

'Lady Muck,' Grace said. They walked on, fast. She didn't ask any more questions. They went back to the ship. They had two more days ashore together before the engine-room repair was completed, a little ahead of the Chief Engineer's estimate. Five days after entry the *Orvega* cleared away south for the River Plate.

Bolsover, the *estancia* manager, was a drinker, though not in the same bracket as Tidy, who largely sulked in his cabin now that his tap had been turned off by

118

order of the Captain. No steward would take the risk of supplying him, not even when offered money. Bolsover, however, was easy; he had no scruples and he sympathized with Tidy. The loss of his wife, the loss of his booze, a double blow. Bolsover took a bottle of whisky along to Tidy's cabin and allowed Tidy to gloom.

Tidy talked about his wife; he was still devastated. By now a cable had come from the son. What had been intended as the voyage of a lifetime had turned to ashes, but at least he would soon be with his son and his family.

The levels in the whisky glasses fell; the glasses were replenished time and again. Tidy repeated his various comments on Lady Moyra Bentinck, the architect of his officially alcohol-free state. Bitch, whore, adulteress, stuck-up old trout.

'You're probably right,' Bolsover said. It did go on, undoubtedly. There was usually a fair amount of high-class fornication going on around the *estancias* of South America, though admittedly mainly on the part of the men, who tended to make use of their *droit de seigneur*, the female workers having little choice in the matter.

'Of course I'm right,' Tidy said.

'Sure you are, ol' chap.' Bolsover hiccuped. 'Better to forget it now, though. You've, well, had your say.' Which was putting it mildly. 'Don't want to get into more trouble with the skipper.'

'Bugger the skipper. Look what the sod did to me.'

'True. But look on the bright side, why not? You're not doing too badly right now, are you, eh?'

Tidy nodded; maudlin tears came to his eyes. 'You're a decent fellow...ol' fellow,' he said thickly. 'Can't thank you enough.'

'Thass awright.'

The bottle grew steadily empty. Bolsover regarded it sadly.

'Got another in my cabin,' he said. 'I'll go and get it. Can't stop the party now.'

Bolsover lurched along to his cabin, fending himself off the alleyway bulkheads as the ship rolled.

Patience was taking a new approach: having seen Chatto with a female passenger ashore, he had reached the conclusion that to be found in a compromising situation might well force his intended victim's hand. Patience knew the moral outlook of the passenger companies' management. And though he had had no personal experience of sailing as an officer in the steamships, he knew enough about the sea life to know that a deck officer, whose accommodation was beneath the bridge, beneath the quarters of the Captain and Chief Officer, would scarcely risk taking a woman to his own cabin. *Ergo,* the woman's cabin would constitute the rendezvous.

This time, Patience was more circumspect. In his baggage he had one decent suit and a clean shirt with starched cuffs and a starched collar. These he put on in the close stuffiness of his twelve-berth cabin before once again hopping nocturnally over the barriers between the classes. A prowling nightwatchman was unlikely to query a well-dressed passenger; and there was no rule prohibiting the passengers walking around the ship at night, no rule to prevent them visiting other cabins.

The overriding problem was that Patience had no idea of either the name of Chatto's woman or the whereabouts of her cabin. This was, undoubtedly, a very considerable obstacle. But a reconnaissance might produce something. There would very likely be a cabin list posted outside the purser's office, for instance, and a process of elimination might provide answers. A female, travelling on her own in a single-berth cabin—you didn't have sexual relations with a woman whose husband was aboard, that was just common sense—that would at least narrow it down. There wouldn't be many women travelling alone to South American ports.

Patience made his way along the first-class alleyways, heading for the main lobby where the purser's office was situated, keeping an eye open for the master-at-arms or his subordinates.

Ahead of him in the starboard alleyway a figure missed its footing, fell in a heap and said, 'Bugger.' Patience recognized insobriety when he met it. Avoiding a scene, he turned back along the alleyway but was brought up all standing by a shout.

'Hey, you, bloke. Gimme a hand, eh?'

Patience cursed under his breath. But the best way to avoid further noise was to oblige. This he did. He hauled Bolsover to his feet, found that the man was carrying a full bottle of whisky.

'Many thanks, bloke,' Bolsover said somewhat indistinctly. He steadied himself against the bulkhead. 'One good turn deserves another, so they say. Care to join us in a little celebration?'

Why not? Any first-class passenger would at least be aware of the ship's Second Officer. There might be gossip: it wasn't all that easy to keep yourself to yourself at sea.

Patience had not, formerly, been much of a drinker. As First Mate of a windjammer you had to watch your step in that direction. At the end of each voyage, the Master was obliged to render to the Owners a report on each of his officers, a report giving his opinion on their seamanship capability, their overall efficiency or lack of it, and their character. This report always included a statement as to whether they were of sober habit or not.

These days, Patience was prepared to drink with any man, the more so if he didn't have to pay for it himself. He found Bolsover and Tidy convivial. Convivial, drunk, and forthcoming.

'Second Officer—name of Chatto. Course we know him. We're at his table. The both of us, right, Mr Tidy?'

Tidy murmured something indistinct: he

was drooling at the corners of his mouth by this time.

'Decent young chap,' Bolsover said. 'Where did you know him, then?'

'I don't know him directly,' Patience said. 'Friend of mine said he was aboard the *Orvega.*' He had already explained, or invented, his own position: first-class passenger, name of Smith which was safe enough, confined to his cabin with a bad go of lumbago, which was why they hadn't seen him around before.

'All the way out from Liverpool?' Bolsover asked.

'All the way out from Liverpool.' It wasn't really important; these two were well enough away not to be feeling much pain. 'But as I was saying...young Chatto. I told my friend I'd contact him. Not had a chance yet.' He paused. 'I did overhear something. Found himself a lady friend.' He gave a wink. 'We all need our oats. No harm in that.'

'Course not. But Chatto...I've had a yarn or two with him. Shared interest in an *estancia.* I doubt if he's interested in a lady friend aboard. Not seeing what he's aiming for in the long run.'

'Uh huh.' Patience was careful not to

show too much interest. More whisky was poured. It would all emerge before long. Bolsover looked the expansive sort, the sort that enjoyed a gossip. And a scandal.

A voicepipe whined on the bridge. Tom answered, 'Second Officer here.'

The call was from aft, a nightwatchman. There was alarm in his voice, an urgency. 'Fire aft, sir-'

'Where, exactly?'

'Steerage accommodation, F deck. Straw mattresses caught alight.'

'Very good. Rouse out the master-at-arms and the fire parties pronto. I'll have more hands down as soon as possible. Start getting the passengers out on deck.' Tom rammed the voicepipe cover down, then called the Captain and the engine room. He passed orders down via the bridge messenger to the bosun. All Hands was the watchword now. Fullbright reached the bridge within thirty seconds, pulling his monkey jacket over his pyjamas. The fire parties began to assemble, the fire hoses were run out by the stewards who in emergency formed the firefighters in the passenger accommodation.

Tom was ordered below to assist the

Chief and First Officers. The Fourth Officer came to the bridge to replace him. Fullbright's face was drawn with anxiety: fire at sea was just about the worst calamity, potentially, that could come to any shipmaster. Before now, careers had come to grief on the terrible rock of fire.

Tom raced below, sliding down the handrails of the accommodation ladders, feet scarcely touching the treads. In the after decks the passengers stood in groups, panic-stricken, the women clutching their children, the menfolk trying to comfort them. The master-at-arms and his staff were inside the steerage, trying to control those who had not yet made it out on the open deck, herding them to the doors and comparative safety on the port and starboard sides. Thick clouds of smoke were billowing from the doors and through this smoke Tom could see the red flicker of flame as the woodwork of the cabins caught.

He found the master-at-arms. It appeared that some of the passengers were trapped, unable or unwilling to cross a barrier of fire. There were believed to be children among them.

Tom went through the starboard door,

a seawater-soaked handkerchief pressed to his mouth and nose. He knew the ship's geography. The smoke was too thick for him to keep his eyes open, but he could move by touch.

By now the whole ship had been roused out. Harrison and his engineers were standing by in the engine and boiler rooms and at the pumping stations to keep up the pressure on the fire hoses. A watch was being kept on the holds, although the *Orvega's* cargo of machine parts was unlikely to catch fire. In the purser's office the assistant pursers emptied the money from the safe into canvas bags: if they should have to take to the boats, the Owners would expect a full accounting of the cash. The first- and second-class passengers, scantily dressed, crowded the lounges in their sections. The stench of the burning straw was spreading; the feeling was one of fear. Through the big square ports of the first-class lounge, the seamen could be seen casting off the gripes of the lifeboats and swinging them out to be lowered on the falls to the embarkation deck. Inside the lounge, Lady Moyra Bentinck sat huddled in a corner, trying to hide her bulk. Bitch, whore and so on...she almost saw death as preferable to such dishonour.

Bolsover and his cronies were rudely interrupted. The boozing party was broken up by the steward who thundered on the cabin door with peremptory orders to get up on deck. Tidy and Bolsover sat now in the first-class lounge, awaiting the next order from the bridge, the order to go to their boat stations.

Patience made his way fast and unchallenged back to the steerage. Whatever else he might be, Patience was no coward, and the inbred instincts of the sea held good.

SEVEN

The engines had been stopped to reduce the wind effect; for the same reason the bell-mouthed ventilators on deck had been turned with their backs to the wind. Men, women and children continued to stream from the port and starboard doors of the accommodation, pushing, trampling, cursing, terrorized to a high degree of

Me First. In some cases the seamen were forced to use their fists to protect the children and the old people.

Patience entered the after-cabin flats by means of a companion ladder for'ard of the main exit doors to the open deck, bringing himself close to the seat of the fire. The smoke here was thick, the heat intense. Patience stumbled over passengers overcome by the smoke, lying helpless on the deck. He picked one woman up, pushed her ahead of himself, urging on what had become a mob, a slow stampede making for the open decks. Others, members of the ship's crew, were with him now. A moment later a stream of water knocked Patience off his feet. Steam billowed as he dragged himself to his feet with his burden, bruised by the heavy tread of the passengers, blood running from a cut on his head. He was aware, as he neared the starboard door and the smoke thinned, of Chatto behind him, making his way along with two small children held in his arms.

Out on deck he gasped for breath, taking in great gulps of air. He felt sick, dizzy. He was no longer young; and not so fit as he'd once been.

The hands worked throughout what was left of the night. As dawn came up, the fire hoses had had their effect: the blaze was under control, the fires out though smouldering continued until virtually the whole of the after accommodation was waterlogged and swimming with burnt debris. It was a shambles, smelling strongly of the burnt straw and woodwork. But there was a bright side to calamity: when the roll of passengers was called by the second steward, no one was missing. A large sick-list of burns cases and those affected by the smoke—work for the doctor and nursing sister—but no deaths.

'A miracle,' Fullbright said when the report was brought to him on the bridge. Through his mind ran a line from the seaman's hymn: *For those in peril on the sea*. To Fullbright, God's hand was clearly seen. But nevertheless there were now immense problems, chief among them how to rehabilitate the steerage passengers deprived of their accommodation and belongings. Improvization was called for until a more permanent arrangement could be made at Buenos Aires, still some days ahead. The ship was now faced with a probably long delay in the River Plate and a consequent very late arrival in Valparaiso. In the interval there would have to be an inquiry into the cause of the fire for inclusion in the Captain's report to the company in Liverpool. It was, in fact, almost a foregone conclusion that someone had, against the steerage regulations, smoked in his cabin. Donkeys' breakfasts—straw palliasses—didn't take kindly to pipes and matches.

With the ship once again under way, Fullbright called a conference in his day cabin: Chief Officer, Chief Engineer, purser, doctor, chief and second stewards. Fullbright was concerned principally with the passengers' welfare: the Chief Officer and the carpenter had reported the ship seaworthy so there were no worries in that direction, and Dr Murphy reported that those passengers and crew with burns and smoke-inhalation problems were not likely to succumb. There were some broken limbs sustained in the rush and crush and these were being dealt with satisfactorily.

'We're going to have to cause upset and friction,' the Captain said, 'but they'll have to put up with it.' He paused. 'I'll put that in plain language: the steerage passengers will have to use the first- and second-class lounges—and I don't mean just for sitting around in. They'll have to sleep there. Blankets must be provided, and so on...and in some cases, the old perhaps, and any sick—they'll have to be accommodated in the spare cabins. You'll see to that, Purser.'

'Yes, sir.'

'You, Hardy,' Fullbright went on, addressing the chief steward, 'will have to work out the feeding arrangements with the head waiters. Another thought,' he added, 'about cabins. If the spare cabins aren't enough, I shall ask my officers to put their cabins at the general disposal. My own quarters will be available likewise. It'll not be easy or comfortable for anybody, but this is a time to show...well, let's call it humanity.'

Patience, recovered from the ordeal, sat in the first-class lounge. He was pleased enough with events. There was more comfort, except perhaps when trying to sleep under a blanket on a bare floor, and there would be the freedom of more deck space in the open air.

There would also be plenty of opportunity

of keeping an eye open for any womanizing on young Chatto's part. Patience didn't like the word blackmail and tried not to think of it in those terms. *Mister* Chatto, Second Mate, beg his pardon, Second Officer...enjoying all the good things of the sea life that were now denied himself: good accommodation, the services of a steward, first-class food, reasonable pay (though the sea was never a provider of wealth), a responsible position in charge of men and eventually the prospect of command, finally perhaps marine superintendent of the Line, a senior Master shore-based in his older years, a wife and family at home. All that was now denied Patience was laid at young Chatto's feet; and he, Patience, had in a sense made it all possible for him. Patience had taught him what he knew about the sea and ships, had formed his upward path for him, shaped him, wrought him into being a seaman. Patience almost saw himself as a guiding light, a nurturer of the young, the maker of Master Mariners. Chatto...money was still important, was still in fact vital, but by now it had become not just the money. Patience had become victim to a consuming jealousy and a vindictive hatred. As he sat there, in the first class as a matter of expediency, not of right, he blamed Chatto for all his misfortunes. And he was going to get even whatever the consequences.

As if in confirmation of Fullbright's prognostications, the spare cabins did not prove sufficient to meet the urgent need of a number of steerage passengers. The ship's officers had been obliged to help out. Tom made over his cabin to a burns case, a young woman with two children, a boy and a girl, the latter with a white, sickly face and a club foot. Tom shifted himself to a shakedown in a corner of the chart room. This he did without complaint; the small family was in a far worse position than himself, and the young husband, himself remaining under a blanket in the second-class lounge, was pathetically grateful.

A few, a very few, of the first-class passengers gave up their cabins for the less fortunate, the burns and limb cases. One to do so was, perhaps surprisingly, the crusty bank manager who, together with his wife and son, moved out into the first-class lounge and its hard lying. Another was Grace Handley, who also shifted to the lounge. This was observed, with annoyance, by Patience. There would be no hanky-panky in public.

Or not too much hanky-panky. There was always the boat deck, available for a passionate kiss and perhaps a little more. You never knew, and anything could be the basis for putting a spoke in Chatto's wheel, so Patience would watch out.

Tom's duties kept him busy. Besides his two daily four-hour bridge watches, there was the navigation, the 'shooting of the sun', the fixing of the ship's position by use of the sextant daily at noon, an exercise which all deck officers from the Sixth Officer to the First Officer were expected to attend; but the responsibility for making, or advising the Captain to make, any alteration to the ship's course and speed as a result of the noon observation was Tom's. He had the responsibility of keeping the ship's chronometers, deep down in the ship, in working order with a view to total accuracy of time; likewise the accuracy of the magnetic compass, the steering compass on the bridge, now back in use as the main steering position following the repair to the wheel. As Second Officer in a ship carrying the royal mails, he was also in charge of the mail room and its security, and this involved daily and thorough checks and never mind the fact that the mail room was kept securely locked at all times, with the key lodged in the safe in the Captain's sleeping cabin.

However, none of this precluded a little socializing.

And, as Patience had thought to himself, there was always the boat deck, the shadow of the lifeboats. But the closer the ship came to the River Plate, the more Tom's thoughts turned towards Dolores Pontarena.

Mr Tidy had not sacrificed his cabin and no pressure had been applied to get him to do so. His grieving was respected. Further private drinking sessions took place, with Bolsover and sometimes Patience. They had all become friends. Before the fire had brought that first session to a sudden close, Patience had learned of the Pontarena *estancia* and Tom's friendship with one of the daughters. Now, a day or so off the Buenos Aires arrival, Patience raised the subject again.

'Those people,' he said reflectively. 'The

Pontarenas. Pretty wealthy, I suppose?'

Bolsover nodded. 'Very! Stinking rich. You don't count their holding in acres—hundreds of square miles more like. I reckon it's the biggest in the Argentine. Lavish life style, dozens of house servants, estate labourers, polo ponies, the lot. Makes your mouth water.'

'Yes. And some of the wealth rubs off on the daughters, of course.'

'Probably. I reckon they live the high life all right, and when old man Pontarena pops off, well, they'll be really in the money.' Bolsover emptied his whisky glass and refilled it from the open bottle. 'I believe Señor Pontarena regrets the lack of a son. Three daughters...which means he'll have his eye on the right kinds of sons-in-law.'

'That's right,' Patience said. Old man Pontarena was likely to be particular in that respect. Chatto, Patience forced himself to concede, would probably be acceptable. A well-set-up man, good-looking, hard-working, loyal and honest, just the man, probably, to impress an *estancia* owner without a son to take over. It would mean leaving the sea, of course, which Chatto might not be prepared to do. But Patience knew that many a seaman had over the years been wooed away from the sea's undoubtedly hard life and long absences from home and family by the delights of wealth and easy living in South America.

But spokes in the wheel could well put an end to such happy dreams. Reflectively, Patience held out his glass.

Two mornings later, under a many-coloured dawn, the *Orvega* stopped engines off the mouth of the River Plate and flew the signal for a pilot. With the pilot embarked, the ship proceeded to the north entry channel, with leadsmen in the chains taking continual soundings. Fullbright saw dredgers working in the south channel: both channels were tricky for a deep-draught ship, and the Buenos Aires arrival was always a time of some anxiety for the Masters on the South American run.

Fullbright breathed easy as the *Orvega* nosed into the berth at the Puerto Madero. Orders were passed fore and aft for the securing lines to be hauled through the fairleads and made fast to the shore bollards. The pilot took his leave and the Captain passed an order to the Officer of the Watch.

'Finished with engines, Mr Attenbury.'

The telegraph handles were hauled over, bells rang and were repeated back from the engine room. On the starting platform the Chief Engineer eased his uniform cap from his head, wiped sweat from his face with a bunch of cotton-waste, and handed over to his Second Engineer.

Immediately on arrival the PSNC's agent had come aboard with the other port officials to inspect the burnt out steerage accommodation. With him was the manager of the repair yard; after a first inspection the manager estimated a fourteen-day job to make the spaces fit for living in.

'More or less,' he said. 'It won't be comfortable, but it'll be good enough to finish the voyage. You'll get the job finished off in Valparaiso.'

That had to be good enough. Fullbright didn't want more delay than was absolutely essential. He had yet to take his ship round Cape Horn, and the longer the delay the more the likelihood of worsening weather conditions. With a fourteen-day port period, shore leave was easy enough to secure. But a disappointment awaited Tom. The PSNC agent had brought a message from Señorita Dolores Pontarena: she was unable to get to Buenos Aires. Her father was ill; he had taken a bad fall from his horse while riding round his estates, had been unconscious for a while and was now laid up with a broken leg.

That was all; no hint of when or where they might meet again and no particular apology, just the bare facts. Tom was more than disappointed. He could sympathize with the father's bad luck, but he seemed to detect a coldness, a lack of interest. There were, after all, two other daughters and Señor Pontarena was evidently by no means at death's door.

Somewhat mutinously, Tom looked elsewhere for companionship during the long stay in port, and it became inevitable that it was Grace Handley to whom he turned.

She didn't ask any questions, though she could see well enough that something was wrong, that Tom was upset. She accepted a stroke of luck and determined to make the most of it. They went ashore as they had done in Rio de Janeiro but this time went together down the gangway. They walked into the city, along the streets that, like

Manhattan in New York, intersected at right angles making a pattern of uniformity; they strolled the wide boulevards and the palm-fringed squares, admired the Statue of Liberty in the Plaza de la Victoria, the Casa Rosada, the university, the cathedral, the opera house; they sat in Palermo Park, on the banks of the Plate, visited the zoological gardens.

Tom had overnight leave. They talked about this; Grace made the overtures, dangled temptation. Tom was human enough; and he was feeling rather badly let down. There were hotels in Buenos Aires where no questions would be asked and in any case Grace Handley was wearing a wedding ring. But Tom's heart wouldn't let him do it. The hour was late and they would stay in a hotel, but in separate bedrooms.

The steerage accommodation would perforce remain unusable while the work went on. Ainsworth represented to the Captain that the first- and second-class passengers wouldn't wear the interruption to their comfort throughout the enforced stay; Buenos Aires, despite its name—'Good Air'—was an airless place, the climate

141

was humid, the temperature still high even though it was now late summer. The overcrowding was much on Fullbright's mind; he was in agreement with the purser that an alternative must be found. The agent took over the task, and that afternoon he announced that he had arranged for the steerage passengers to be moved en masse to hostel accommodation in what was admittedly a rundown district of the city, an area that had not been rebuilt over recent years as had the more central parts.

He spoke to the Captain. 'There'll be complaints, but really they're lucky to be off the ship. I suppose you've sniffed the air, Captain? The weather, I mean.'

'I smell a *pampero*, Señor Mendoza.' The pamperos were basically dust storms and the wind could be strong and often accompanied by tropical thunderstorms that could be dangerous; but the blown dust was the worst aspect. All ventilators, ports and intakes would have to be closed or the ship's interior could begin to resemble a dust bowl, or desert. All in all, the shore was probably a better prospect.

The steerage was duly informed by the

purser. A little before night came down, open horse-drawn wagons drew up on the dockside and the displaced passengers disembarked. It was a pathetic sight. There seemed to be not a spare garment between them all, scarcely any baggage, and almost certainly very little money. At Fullbright's request, the agent would make arrangements by cable with Liverpool for some cash to be disbursed and charged, along with the hostel accommodation, to the Line's account. Their predicament was far from being of their own making—except for one man, the pipe-smoker who had caused it. This man had already been brought before the Captain, and had been handed into custody of the local police to be charged with endangering life and property at sea.

Patience looked around at the strictly functional rooms of the hostel, disliking what he saw, though in all conscience it was probably better than the steerage decks. A thin carpet, thin almost to threadbareness, covered the floor of the communal lounge; potted palms loomed in corners, their leaves dry, dusty and sad-looking, yellowish with neglect. The dormitories were bleak, the washing and lavatory facilities scanty. Long queues of men and women had already formed. Children whined incessantly, it seemed, squeezing their legs together in agony. In several cases the wait had proved too long, and pools had formed, adding embarrassment to the parents' woes. The place smelled of urine, sweat, unwashed bodies, dirty clothing and malfunctioning drains.

Patience contained his loathing as best he could, waiting for morning. The passengers had been informed of the likely cash disbursement, and Patience would be early in the queue at the agent's offices.

The *pampero* struck before Fullbright had expected it. It came in the early hours of the next morning, announced by an almighty clap of thunder that seemed to rock the liner at its berth. At that first clap the hands were roused out, the stewards included. All intakes were closed just in time, before the great swirls of dust blew up from the dry land to encase the ship. Even with the intakes secured, that dust penetrated. It went into the cabins and alleyways, dry and gritty. It went into Lady Moyra Bentinck's stateroom, an unpleasant fact for which she blamed her maid, a girl from the west of Ireland brought for Her Ladyship's comfort from her house in Eaton Square.

'The window should have been shut before I went to bed, Connolly.'

'I'm sorry, me lady.'

'You may well be. Start clearing up the dust. I can't be expected to sleep in this. It's *too* much.'

'Yes, me lady.'

Lady Moyra scowled. The Irish, the Catholic Irish, were peasants, sluts. Lady Moyra regretted the girl's company, but needs must...for some reason or other, servants never stayed. It was very inconvenient. Possibly a better maid might be found in Valparaiso, and if so then Connolly could pay her own way back to Letterkenny or wherever it was. For her part Mary Connolly bore her depressing lot, wielded dustpan and brush unavailingly, and consoled herself with hating her dreadful mistress and remembering an apocryphal story told her by a young footman at the London house. There had been an overbearing English mistress of an Irish girl from the bogs of Connemara, employed as a general servant in a small house in Kingstown, County Dublin. This mistress had taken pains to instruct the girl, whose first place in service this was, in English manners. She was always, for instance, to answer 'Yes, ma'am' or 'No, ma'am' as appropriate when spoken to. Also, if a visitor should ask if he or she might—for instance—take the dog for a walk, she was to answer 'Yes, ma'am (or sir), do if you please.' The 'if you please' was very important. One night the good lady gave a dinner party, to be cooked by the Irish girl. A string of confusing and contradictory instructions was issued; the poor girl became terribly agitated; and into the gathering of guests she came for advice. She stood trembling in the doorway of the drawing-room and said, 'Yes, ma'am—no, ma'am—do if you please...is it up the duck's arse I should stuff the green peas?'

Mary Connolly would have relished a repeat performance here and now, and bad cess to the old bitch, whom she had quite clearly heard called a whore, which was probably correct, though you'd never think it to look at her. Who would want her, for heaven's sake?

146

The thunder had shaken the hotel, seeming to be right overhead. Lightning had crackled outside. There was a shatter of wind against Tom's windows. There was a sound like rain; but Tom had experienced the *pampero* when in sail, and recognized the sound of grit slammed by the increasing wind.

Grace Handley had been scared during the night. They met at breakfast and Tom reassured her. There had been nothing to worry about except that they might find the ship filled with dust when they returned aboard.

Nothing to worry about. But when they left the hotel for Tom to return aboard for a day's duty, Patience was walking along the road outside.

EIGHT

Patience had seen them. It was a stroke of luck, very unexpected. He had been on his way to the agent's office, which was just around the corner from the hotel, to draw his cash disbursement. It was obvious the pair had seen him, but they had evidently not been sure he had seen them; they had turned about and gone inside, a useless precaution but proof positive.

However, Patience decided to make quite sure. Having drawn his money—five pounds in Argentine currency, a fair enough sum—he went back to the hotel, reaching it some half-hour after Chatto and his woman could be presumed to have left. He went to Reception and spoke to the clerk. A Mr Chatto and a Mrs Handley had stayed overnight, giving their address as the *Orvega*. Handley? The clerk had been quite certain that the lady's name had been Handley. He was emphatic that they had been the only guests from the port-bound *Orvega*.

Handley. Patience would check that with the passenger list. He would do that straight away; he was himself a passenger and had every right to go back aboard even though currently accommodated ashore. And it was going to be useful to confirm the woman's name, and as a result get her cabin number. The fact that they had not shared a room was no matter. They were compromised.

People could move from one room to another.

Grace had wanted to know why Tom had pulled her back into the hotel. He had said something about being seen by a passenger. She was amazed at his concern. 'We're not aboard the ship, Tom. Does it really matter?'

Tom was remembering, had never forgotten, Patience's threat. There was no knowing what the man might do. Tom was thinking of Dolores Pontarena. He might have condemned her too far in his mind. The father could have been worse than the bare message had revealed. That sight of Patience had brought him up with a round turn, confirming that he had been right not to yield to temptation. Grace Handley could never be anything in the long run but a ship that passed in the night. She was a married woman, unlikely to be granted a divorce by her husband.

Though innocent, there was a nasty taste. It had left Tom feeling at odds with himself. The whole thing had taken on a shady aspect. He cursed the horse that had thrown Señor Pontarena.

Answering Grace's question he said,

'Well, never mind. It doesn't matter, no.'

The *pampero* had blown itself out, but the ship was still suffering the effects of the dust, and of the lightning too. The foretopmast had been struck; the lightning conductor had taken the brunt, but the wireless transmitting and receiving aerials had been badly damaged. The wireless operators were aloft, seeing what was to be done. Fullbright wanted no further delay in the ship's schedule. There were thirteen days to go and that should be more than enough. Fullbright, remembering his years in the windjammers, years when a man going to sea was out of contact with the shore, with the Owners, with home and family, with everything except the ship and God, was not worried about taking the *Orvega* out of harbour without wireless. But in that he was not the final arbiter. Present-day regulations stipulated that, wireless telegraphy having been invented, all passenger ships must carry it.

The purser was on the promenade deck, looking down at the dockside and the wagonloads of timber waiting to come aboard for the use of the carpenters, when

Tom Chatto came up the gangway. He was alone; prudence had dictated that Grace Handley should remain ashore until a more reasonable hour. But her absence from her cabin had been noted: her stewardess reported to the purser's staff that her bunk had not been slept in. Ainsworth, when he heard this, shrugged it off. Any passenger was entitled to spend a night ashore and when the ship was tied up for a full due it was not surprising if they did so. Nevertheless, young Chatto had come aboard very bright and early and, recalling that previous conversation with Mrs Handley, Ainsworth was inclined to put two and two together. Also, there had been stray items of gossip. He hoped Chatto knew what he was doing. The time might well come when temporary liaisons would be commonplace; but that time had not yet arrived and great discretion was called for.

Two days before the repairs to the steerage accommodation were scheduled to complete, a cable reached Tom via the purser's office. Dolores Pontarena would after all be coming to Buenos Aires. She would stay with the aunt whose address was given in the cable, which didn't go into details as to how Dolores was after all able to leave her father. Tom was now in a quandary: he remembered something the old sea-dog Uncle Benjamin had once told him: in the Queen's ships, when at sea on Saturday nights, a certain toast was always drunk by the wardroom officers at dinner: 'Sweethearts and wives, and may they never meet.'

Grace Handley was going to have her nose put out of joint. Tom had as yet had no experience of women's jealousy, but he did have imagination. And there was something about Grace that told him she had a temper hidden away somewhere.

During the day of the cable's arrival she managed to get some of the facts out of him. It couldn't be avoided. He had gone ashore and telephoned the aunt; Dolores would arrive that evening, and he was invited to dinner.

'You're what I call a two-timer, Tom.'

He flushed: there was truth in that and he had to face it. 'I'm sorry,' he said. 'I mean that...but—'

'But what?'

He said lamely, 'It was never meant to

be anything permanent. I thought we both understood that.'

'Yes. I'm not thinking about myself, Tom. Hasn't it occurred to you that the girl might be hurt?'

It had; he admitted it. His only excuse, he had also to admit to himself, was what the eye didn't see... However, Grace dropped the subject, and went away, leaving him standing on the boat deck. He was relieved that there hadn't been a scene.

That evening Tom went ashore, making for the aunt's house in a suburb of the city—Belgrano, a journey by horse-drawn cab of some five miles. He had a strong feeling that he was to be vetted and reported upon. With Grace Handley in mind this was an uneasy feeling. He was not reassured by the appearance of the aunt, Señorita Concepcion Garcia, aged at a guess around sixty-five. This virginal old lady was a reasonable replica of Queen Victoria: round, short, white hair in a bun at the back of her neck and head covered with a piece of white lace. Her manner was regal; and Dolores not having yet arrived, Tom was subjected to a preliminary appraisal and catechism.

'Your family, they are Irish?'

Tom nodded, sitting in a well-upholstered armchair in the señorita's drawing-room, which was sumptuously furnished—the house was large, what Dolores had referred to as a *quinta*, almost a country estate. Tom answered many probing questions, receiving a noncommittal nod each time. He described life in the deanery, spoke of his interests, his love of an open-air life and of the sea.

'The sea, yes. You have a good career, Señor Chatto?'

'I think so, yes, Señorita Garcia.'

She didn't comment; she spoke of Dolores, a favourite niece. She told him that her brother-in-law, Señor Pontarena, was still confined to bed but had relented and allowed Dolores to come to her in Belgrano. After that, conversation seemed to flag. Sherry had been brought by a manservant and now they toyed with their glasses. Señorita Garcia broke the silence suddenly. 'Dolores, she is late.'

Tom had had similar thoughts. He had been growing uncomfortable under the inquisition.

Time passed; the aunt was beginning to worry. So was Tom. Dolores, the aunt

154

said, was coming by train, the Buenos Aires Great Southern Railway, from Bahia Blanca. From the railway station she would come to Belgrano by cab. Surely nothing could go wrong.

In the city there had been a reunion of a sort. Bolsover had taken Tidy under his wing. Tidy was, naturally, grieving for his wife and needed taking out of himself. Bolsover had suggested they go ashore. A change of scene would be good, and there was no point in moping about the ship. Tidy, a little unsober, had been persuaded. Tidy asked about the friend they knew as Sivyer, known to be accommodated in the shoreside hostel.

'We'll get in touch,' Bolsover said. 'The purser'll know the address.' He went along to the purser's office, spoke to an assistant purser who proved helpful. The pair went ashore, found Patience sitting gloomily in the lounge of the hostel: he was glad enough to see them.

'There's a bar close by,' he said. 'Not up to much, but not too bad.'

They went to this bar, through the sleazy streets and the throngs of poorly dressed locals. Tidy and Patience drank brandy.

Bolsover settled for whisky. He had a strong feeling that Patience expected to have his drinks paid for, but what the hell, the man had seemed down on his luck. Patience began to grow drunk. Drunk and, like Tidy, maudlin. He seemed to be nursing some sort of vendetta against the ship's Second Officer. Bolsover remembered that Patience had harped on about Chatto earlier, aboard the liner.

'What's the gripe?' he asked.

'Young bastard,' Patience said spitefully. He nursed his brandy glass, glaring at the other occupants of the bar, a ruffianly lot of swarthy, mustachioed men plus a number of obvious prostitutes. 'You told me about that Pontarena,' he said to Bolsover.

'Yes. So?'

'Him and Chatto. Or his daughter and Chatto. Know anything about that, do you?'

'Not a thing. Why?'

'Any of the Pontarena family here in Buenos Aires?'

Bolsover scratched his head. 'I believe there's a sister-in-law, out Belgrano way... matter of fact I know there is. Señorita Garcia. My boss sent me down here a year or so back with some sale papers for her to sign.'

'Belgrano.' Patience seemed to chew the word over, then said, 'You'll know her address, then.'

Bolsover gave him a searching look. 'Not offhand. Anyway, it's not up to me to give it away.'

'I thought,' Patience said, 'you were a friend.'

'So I am. But it'd be more than my job's worth...and anyway, I wouldn't. What do you want with the old lady?'

'Not your business.' Patience got to his feet, unsteadily. He finished what remained of his brandy, then lurched out of the bar. Bolsover looked at Tidy. He didn't like it, he said. Patience had had a sort of lunatic look about him. However, as the man had said, it wasn't his business...

'Back to the ship,' he said. It hadn't been a very good idea to rope in Patience for a drinking session.

Patience nagged. Patience was obsessed with something.

Señorita Garcia. A common enough name and there could be others in Belgrano. But this one was almost certainly very wealthy since she was a kinswoman of the Pontarenas, that lot with estates measured, according to Bolsover, in hundreds of square miles. Patience had time on his hands and somebody in that suburb, Belgrano, would know of her, that was certain enough. Go and find out? Patience made some inquiries after leaving the bar, lurching up to a man on a street corner. Belgrano was all of five miles, a long walk. Patience, with some confused idea in mind that this Señorita Garcia could be persuaded to part with money in return for information about Mister Chatto—real money, for she would naturally wish to keep the family clean—started walking.

A small shop in Belgrano proved helpful. Patience was given directions. He found the house after darkness had set in. A large house set in spacious grounds, at the end of a long drive flanked by luxuriant hibiscus hedges.

He was about to walk up the drive when he heard the sound of horse's hoofs. A cab came into sight, turning to enter the drive. Patience was outlined for a moment in the glow from the cab's flickering lamp. The moon was also giving its light; in this Patience saw the girl sitting in the cab. Chatto's woman? Something snapped in Patience's brain. Chatto, the cause of his misfortunes. As the cab slowed, he jumped for the horse's head. The animal reared, snorted. Unseated by the sudden jolt, the cab driver catapulted from his box, crashed headfirst on to the gravel and lay still. Patience ran for the door and opened it. He lurched over the step and got his hands round the neck of the girl just as she gave a high scream. The scream unnerved Patience, brought him to a realization of what he was doing. He let go of the girl's throat, muttered an oath, almost one of apology, and ran off into the darkness. The scream also unnerved the horse: it bolted with the cab.

NINE

There was worry in the aunt's house now. Señorita Garcia seemed not to know what to do. A cable to Señor Pontarena, to confirm that Dolores had left? But if she had not, word would certainly have been sent.

Tom saw that it was up to him. He said he would run back along the road leading from the railway station. It was all he could do, and if the cab had come to grief along the way he would find it. He made a quick find at the bottom of the drive: a man, a cab driver, staggering to his feet, his head bloody. The man was incoherent, managing to get across only the fact that someone had stopped his horse. The police were summoned, a search was made of the district. Ultimately a smashed, horseless cab was found overturned on a country road some miles from Belgrano, an unconscious girl inside.

Dolores was brought to her aunt's house and a doctor was summoned. Soon after, she was able to speak, tearfully. She was able to give a fair description of her attacker.

Patience. Patience in Tom's mind. But without further evidence Tom could do nothing. And with the *Orvega* now close to sailing for Cape Horn and Valparaiso, Tom was required back aboard.

The *Orvega* left Buenos Aires with the repairs, including the *pampero*-damaged wireless aerials, completed on time and the steerage passengers re-embarked. Patience, if it had been Patience, had got away with it. The police had drawn a blank. Tom left the port with many questions unanswered: Dolores, although making a recovery, had been *distraite* and the situation had not been advanced in any direction although Tom believed he had made a reasonably good impression on the aunt. Valparaiso, still many sea-miles ahead, would be the liner's turn-round port and she would remain there for some while; more permanent repairs would be needed before the homeward-bound embarkation for Liverpool. There would be messages waiting in Valparaiso; it was possible, if Tom could get leave, that he might be invited to the *estancia*. More goods on approval, as it were.

Tidy and Bolsover maintained their cabin drinking sessions. Patience had stopped attending. He was aware that he had shot his mouth off a little too much in that bar back in Buenos Aires. And this had not been lost on his erstwhile companions. The newspapers had made much of the police search for Dolores's attacker and the connection, via Tom, with the *Orvega*. Before the liner had left, Bolsover found himself with a split mind: should he take certain suspicions to the police, or should he not? Patience had quite openly wanted to know about the aunt; he had quite brazenly tried to prise out the old lady's address. And he had been very drunk. There was circumstantial evidence, but nothing definite. And Bolsover's boss wouldn't relish his name, and by inference the name of the *estancia* managed by Bolsover, being dragged through the mud of assault and battery and general dirtiness as a result of a boozing session in the sleazier parts of Buenos Aires.

But Bolsover wouldn't forget. Moreover, Patience knew that he wouldn't.

Three days out from the Plate the weather began to deteriorate. The barometric pressure dropped, heavy cloud came in from the south-east as the liner followed her track between the Falkland Islands and the southern extremity of the Argentine coast. Gone were the balmy days of sunshine, heat and blue water. The sea was now grey and ruffled, the wind was cold. There was no pleasure on the open decks; the passengers huddled in the lounges, bars and smoking rooms, grateful for the cups of hot soup brought daily by the stewards at 11.00 a.m. Lady Moyra Bentinck, still in voluntary purdah, felt the drop in temperature and the cold fug in the atmosphere and tormented her maid accordingly.

'I would have thought you'd have laid out my warmer underwear, Connolly.'

'I'm sorry, me lady.'

Lady Moyra sighed; it was too bad. Servants never learned; no intelligence. 'Try to think ahead, Connolly. I'm not used to reminding my maids of every detail.'

'No, me lady.'

Lady Moyra clicked her tongue. 'Really, girl, don't just stand there saying No my lady, Yes my lady, I'm sorry my lady—like a parrot. *Do* something.'

'Yes, me lady.'

Drat the girl. Lady Moyra sighed again and gave up. She stared disconsolately through her cabin port at the grey, heaving sea and the spume blown from the wavetops to form a virtual carpet of white. Lady Moyra was lonely, craved someone to whom she could talk, but not, certainly not, Connolly. If it hadn't been for that appalling man Tidy...but he had happened and there was nothing to be done about it. Except perhaps one thing: she could sue him, take him to court for slander. Indeed she had been thinking about that ever since the episode, but there had been the insurmountable obstacle: what the man had said had been, in basis, true. There *had* been that unfortunate lapse years before in South Africa. She blamed the wretched Boers; had it not been for them, she and the brigadier general might never have met.

She looked across at Connolly, engaged now in what she had been told to do, sorting through her mistress's winter woollies. Silently, of course. Servants didn't speak until spoken to; she had managed to drive *that* into the girl's head. It was as well for Lady Moyra's peace of mind that she was no thought-reader.

Quite suddenly, she made a decision. She said, 'My shawl, Connolly. I shall go out on deck.'

Mary Connolly gaped. Some neck! But maybe the old bitch was thinking it was time to brazen things out.

Shawled and bonneted, Lady Moyra left her cabin on her maid's arm.

Shortly after Lady Moyra had ventured into the public eye, there was what looked like trouble in the fo'c'sle. A man emerged from the weather door leading into the seamen's accommodation, shouting out for the bosun. As Tom looked down from the bridge, Bosun Halloran, working with the donkeyman on the windlass below the break of the fo'c'sle, looked up and ran for the door from which the seaman had emerged. Five minutes later he was seen coming aft, making for the bridge ladder.

On reaching the bridge he reported, 'Man injured, sir. Fell arse over tip down the ladder to the paint store. I've sent for the doctor.'

'Is it serious?' Tom asked.

'I dunno, sir. Could be from the look of it.'

'All right, Bosun. We'll wait for the doctor's report.'

'Yes, sir.' The bosun left the bridge. Tom paced up and down. A seaman injured with the passage of Cape Horn looming was not so great a catastrophe as it would have been aboard a windjammer, but it was certainly unwelcome. Cape Horn was still Cape Horn, and situations could arise in which there would be a

165

call for All Hands. As Tom awaited the doctor's report, the Captain came to the bridge and Tom reported the facts as known.

Fullbright, echoing Tom's own thoughts, said, 'Not good news at this stage. What with being three short already.' His reference was to one of the difficulties suffered by shipmasters often enough: there had been three deserters in Buenos Aires, men who had jumped ship in order to look for a better life in South America, where, at least in the imagination of seafarers fed up with the life afloat, untold riches were there for the taking so long as a man was prepared to work for them on the large estates or in the mines—gold, silver, copper, lead, antimony, coal. In many of the South American ports replacements could be obtained from the boarding-house masters, rapacious individuals who got men drunk—any man would do, seafarer or landsman—and then shanghaied them aboard an outward-bounder short of crew. But Tom knew that Fullbright would never take any part in that sort of trade, nor would the PSNC itself permit it.

Ten minutes later Tom and Fullbright saw the injured seaman being brought aft on the stretcher, going to the ship's surgery. Dr Murphy reported to the Captain shortly after.

'Bad, sir. Compound fractures of both legs. It was a lurch of the ship—'

'And a certain amount of cack-handedness?'

'Probably. Yes, I dare say it was, but the man's in very great pain.'

'I'm not unsympathetic, Doctor, but you know the old saying, one hand for the ship and one for yourself. However, what's to be done about it?'

'I've sedated him, sir. As for treatment...I have to say that it's beyond repair aboard, that is, if the man's to walk and work again.'

'You mean you're suggesting he should be in hospital?'

Murphy nodded. 'That's what I'd like to see, yes.'

'I want this straight, Doctor. In your opinion, it's vital, a case of absolute necessity?'

'Yes, it is.'

Fullbright turned away, paced the bridge, frowning. Then he moved into the chart room. Coming back to the bridge, he said, 'Very well, Doctor. Medical necessity...we're not all that far off the Falklands. I'll deviate into Port Stanley.' He turned to Tom. 'Lay off a course for Cape Pembroke, if you please, Mr Chatto, and let me have an ETA soonest possible. I'll take the bridge watch while you work it out.'

'Aye, aye, sir.' Tom handed over the watch and went into the chart room. As he busied himself with navigational tables and parallel rulers and dividers, he thought: This is turning into a jonah voyage. In more ways than one. Ten minutes later the *Orvega* swung to port on to her new track for the Falklands.

Lady Moyra was going through the starboard-side door to the promenade deck when the ship made her turn; it was a turn across the prevailing wind that took her for a short while across the scend of what by now were quite large waves. The turn caught Lady Moyra at an awkward moment, with one leg over the coaming in the deck and the other leg still inside the bulkhead. She tripped and fell, an undignified sprawl. She screamed loudly. Mary Connolly did her best, trying to lug the inert body up.

'Not that way, you fool. You'll injure me

168

further, can't you see! Oh, the *agony!*'

'I'm sorry, me lady-'

'*Shut up*, do.'

Someone came to their assistance, bending to put his hands beneath Lady Moyra's armpits, and she screamed again. Then she saw who the man was: Tidy.

'Go away, you *vile* man.'

'I'm only—'

'Kindly *leave me alone*. Someone tell the Captain. I can't stand the *agony.*'

She writhed and moaned. Mary Connolly simply didn't know how to cope, so she remained mute until some stewards came from the lounge and one of them went post-haste for the doctor. Since the doctor was busy with the injured seaman, it was Sister Moloney who attended, which didn't please the injured party. Sister Moloney winked at Mary Connolly. Two Irish girls...they both understood each other. It was all a fuss about very little. As, later, Dr Murphy reported to the Captain.

'Bruised bottom, sir.'

'That's all?'

'Well—plus shattered dignity, of course.'

Fullbright grinned. 'Which is not a medical condition, I take it. What are you going to do—about the bottom, I mean?'

'A poultice. A placebo really. It won't do any good but she won't settle for less.'

Tom, who had taken over the watch again, found the incident another pointer to a jonah voyage. Fullbright wasn't going to like having to report to the Owners that his most prized passenger had bruised her bottom. All said and done, the Lady Moyras of this world could use bruised behinds to institute claims against the Company. But at least the old girl was once again off the decks.

The ship was labouring badly now as she made her way easterly for Cape Pembroke and thence Port Stanley. The weather was worsening rapidly, which augured badly for the now delayed passage of Cape Horn. The lurching of the decks, the rise and fall of the bows, made life worse than ever in the steerage section. Beneath the seasick passengers the screw, lifting now and again from the water as the bows dipped under, raced with a shattering vibration that racked the afterdecks. In the surgery the injured seaman suffered even though he had been lashed down against the ship's movement. More sedatives were needed—opium was all that was available. The ship's arrival in Port Stanley was scheduled for some twenty hours ahead. A longish time and one that caused Murphy some anxiety: there was a limit to how much opium could be administered. Murphy and Sister Moloney took it in turns to remain with the man. It made for heavy work, since the seasick passengers in the first and second class clamoured for attention. And, of course, there was always Lady Moyra's bottom to be attended to. She had in the end rejected the poultice and had demanded to be rubbed with some sort of ointment, as she put it; and she wouldn't trust her maid, so Sister Moloney was landed with the job.

Anne Moloney was rebellious. 'There are people in a worse way than you, Lady Moyra.'

'Fiddlesticks. You've *no idea* of the agony I've been through.' Lady Moyra gave a short yelp. 'Don't rub so hard for heaven's sake, girl.'

'Sister, if you don't mind.'

'Mind! I'll tell you what I have got in mind. A report to the Captain. I *will not* put up with impertinence—as you'll find out. Girl.'

Anne Moloney said nothing but she rubbed harder. Lady Moyra, taking the hint, closed her jaws like a trap but remained silent. She would put the girl in her place later on.

At two bells in the forenoon watch next day, the *Orvega* made her arrival off Cape Pembroke and turned south and east to enter Port Stanley, lowering her ensign in salute to the British naval guardship lying off the port. The scene was a bleak one in the extreme, a rocky and barren land, populated mainly by sheep. Signals were exchanged with the warship as Fullbright brought his engines to slow and then stop. He was anxious to be on his way for Cape Horn as soon as possible; even before the way was off the ship a boat was lowered to take Dr Murphy and the stretchered casualty ashore to the hospital, but before Murphy had left the *Orvega* another signal came from the warship. Her Fleet Surgeon would take the case if Fullbright wished; she was leaving for Devonport dockyard in ten days' time, on relief by another battleship, and the injured man could go with her.

This was agreed; the man was lowered into

the boat and, accompanied by Murphy, left the ship. Some half-hour later the doctor returned aboard and the liner headed outwards.

She had cleared East Falkland when there was a sudden escape of steam from the relief valve running up the ship's for'ard funnel, a sound like a waterfall in full spate, with a plume of superheated steam that shot into the sky. Fullbright ran for the engine-room voicepipe, which whistled as he reached it.

'Chief Engineer, sir. All under control.'

'What's happened, Chief?'

Harrison went into a technical explanation: something, which was in fact obvious enough, had blown. 'Will you need shore assistance?' Fullbright asked.

'I don't believe so.' Harrison sounded doubtful, Fullbright thought. 'Not that Port Stanley would be much use anyway,' the Chief Engineer went on. 'The facilities—'

'What about the battleship?'

There was an indeterminate sound at the other end. Harrison said the battleship's engineers could do no better than himself. Professional jealousy? There was always an antagonism between the men who sailed in the merchant ships and those who sailed in the King's ships. But Fullbright knew that Harrison was a first-class engineer and unlikely to have his professional judgment swayed by such considerations. And he himself wanted no further delays; already this voyage had brought its share of them. But he temporized. He said, 'I'll come below, Chief.' He replaced the voicepipe cover and went fast down the starboard ladder, making for the engine room.

TEN

Back on the bridge, Fullbright gave no orders for a return to Port Stanley. Harrison had convinced him; no engineer himself, Fullbright was in Harrison's hands when it came to the technics of modern propulsion. And there was that desire in him to reach Valparaiso without further delay. Delays cost the Owners money; each voyage was on a fairly tight financial rein, yet had to pay its way and make a profit.

So they would continue on passage. That was a responsibility that rested wholly on Fullbright's shoulders, not on the Chief

Engineer. Engineers could advise, never decide policy. All such decisions aboard a ship were those of the Captain.

But Cape Horn lay ahead.

Worry nagged: had the decision been the right one? Tom Chatto, taking over the bridge for his watch later, found the Captain there still, pacing restlessly. They were well clear of the Falklands now—no navigational reason for the Captain's presence. Tom noted the frown, the curt manner. The Old Man was edgy, and Tom could guess why. Before coming on watch he had picked up a rumour emanating from the engineer's mess room: all was not well below, and Harrison was being a wee bit pig-headed.

Chief Officer Forster had nagged in the background ever since his brush with Tom over the latter's timekeeping. It had been nothing specific, just a kind of petty spite, nit-picking as Tom described it to himself.

Now he was at it again.

'Mr Chatto.'

'Yes, sir?'

'The chronometer room.'

'What about it?' Tom was short. Forster had no business to interfere with the chronometers except perhaps in special circumstances.

'Dirt, Mr Chatto. The space is dirty. Not to say filthy.'

'Oh? In what way, Mr Forster?'

'Dust. Dust can get into the chronometers—'

'Very unlikely,' Tom snapped.

'Kindly don't argue with me, Mr Chatto. You will see to it that your yeoman wields his duster and his polishing cloths with more diligence in future or there will be trouble. Clear enough for you, Mr Chatto?'

With that Forster had turned on his heel and marched away, hands clasped behind his back. Angered, Tom went below to the chronometer room. The space was a model of cleanliness. He ran a finger over the casing of the gleaming brass chronometers: it was perfectly clean. A very faint touch of dust showed, such as would appear within minutes of being polished. Tom hissed through his teeth. What was wrong with Forster? Tom believed he had some of the answer to that: Forster was getting on, was a little old to be still a chief officer. Command may be eluding him and he knew it, perhaps. Never to achieve command...to retire without that accolade would naturally be a blow. But there was no need to take out his frustrations on his juniors.

Two days out from Port Stanley the American citizen, Percival J. Bunce, was drinking his bowl of mid-morning soup in the lounge along with Tidy. Tidy had been discussing his *bête noire*, Lady Moyra Bentinck; he was still smarting from having been called a vile man and regretting his impulse to go to the old woman's aid—it had been almost a reflex action, to go to the assistance of any woman in distress, and although she had certainly been distressed, that was no excuse for rudeness.

Tidy had recounted the facts about the dalliance in South Africa; Bunce had heard it all before on the galley wireless but Tidy was the fount, thus worth listening to. Now Tidy said judicially, 'It's not surprising, in a way.'

'How come, Mr Tidy?'

'Well...' Tidy reflected. 'He was a fossilized old bastard. General Bentinck. Not the adulterer.'

'You don't say.'

'Pardon? Yes, I do. I've just said so.'
Tidy rustled irritably. He was unused to
Americanisms. 'A right bastard to his
troops an' all. The old cow...well, she
probably wasn't getting it more than once
a year. Result—natural, really.'

'Uh-huh. Guess you're right at that. The
other guy, the brig—he was different?'

'Yes. Younger like, and what you'd
call handsome. Tall and thin...dark with
it. More hair than the husband, too.
Don't know really what he saw in her,
to be honest.' Tidy was by now using his
imagination to a large extent: he hadn't
been close enough to the nobs to know
what had really gone on, not in detail,
but the knowledge he did have, damning
enough, was giving him cachet, especially
with Bunce who was as nosy as all-
get-out.

'Army life, army life for the officers that
is, tends that way. Specially in India, where
I done time. The mem'sahibs, like, up in
the hill stations with hubby down on the
plains. Ooh-la-la an' all that, comes easy.
And don't look now, Mr Bunce, here she
comes.'

Lady Moyra, recovered from her fall,
had decided to follow up that impulse

178

to show she didn't give a fig for gossip and the sort of low-class persons who spread it. Tidy and Bunce, rather too ostentatiously talking of something else, eyed her furtively. She caught Tidy's eye. He looked away, fast. She marched up to him, her maid holding on to one arm.

'I see you've been talking about me. That will stop, or I shall speak to the Captain.' The hand that was not immobilized by Connolly held a walking stick. This she pointed at the American. 'Who is this person?' she demanded.

Americans were always polite, always friendly. Bunce rose to his feet. 'Pleased to make your acquaintance, ma'am. Percival J. Bunce, ma'am, from Oklahoma. Please call me Percy, ma'am.'

'Call you *what?*' Lady Moyra gave a snort of disgust and prodded at Connolly to get moving.

Tidy said in a low voice, 'You've put your foot in it now an' no mistake.'

'Well, gee whiz, I guess I'm sorry.'

Purser Ainsworth beat a retreat from the counter of the main office. He had seen complaint coming; you could always tell and Lady Moyra was unmistakable, even expected like an unwelcome visitor. Ainsworth left his deputy to deal with her. Or he thought he had.

'I want to see the purser.' Lady Moyra laid the handle of her walking stick on the counter.

'Can I help, Lady Moyra?'

'The purser.'

'But perhaps I—'

'Kindly do as I ask, young man.'

The deputy retreated; Ainsworth was fetched from his office. 'Good morning, Lady Moyra. It's nice to see you up and about again—'

'Never mind that. All I wish to say is that if the passengers continue to *chatter* about me behind my back, which I am convinced is what they *are* doing, then I warn you I shall make a very strong complaint to your agent in Valparaiso for transmission to Sir Murgatroyd Mason-Finch himself. Is that clear?' Lady Moyra turned about and moved away without waiting for an answer. Sir Murgatroyd was the chairman of the Line; Lady Moyra, as Ainsworth was well enough aware, had come aboard with the personal recommendation of the chairman, which made her a very special passenger indeed: Captain's table, bow and scrape, walk away backwards as with royalty. But what could be done about gossip among other passengers? The answer was obvious: nothing at all. But try telling that to Lady Moyra, Ainsworth thought. No doubt Sir Murgatroyd would understand; he was no fool and no bigot either, but if Lady Moyra reported an unsatisfactory voyage, it would rub off on the unfortunate purser, whose job it was to keep everyone happy all the way from departure to arrival.

Lady Moyra was important enough to warrant a report to the Captain, but Ainsworth was reluctant to bother him with domestic problems with the passage of the Horn so close. That, and the engine room. Ainsworth decided on quiet discretion: he ordered his staff, when circulating among the passengers, to utter words of caution; and in particular to silence Messrs Tidy, Bolsover and Bunce. Ainsworth, in common with all experienced pursers, kept his ear close to the ground.

As the *Orvega* dropped south and west from the Falkland Islands, and then altered due west to come between Cape Horn and the icefields of the Antarctic, the wind blew strong and coldness pervaded the ship. There was little exercising now on the boat deck; few passengers braved the promenade decks for their daily constitutional, preferring to sit huddled in their cabins or in the lounges, watching the dead grey sea through the ports. In the steerage there was a chill fug, foetid and nauseous. The passengers sat on the bare wooden benches that formed the steerage lounge, if lounge was the appropriate word for a bleak, uncarpeted space. Patience gloomed, scowled at anyone who approached him. He was in a state of anxiety, anxiety that worsened as the days passed. The fracas back in that Buenos Aires suburb: he might have left some sort of clue behind, he couldn't be absolutely sure. The Pontarena family were people of importance, according to Bolsover. The police were unlikely to let the matter rest. At Valparaiso, he might find himself in trouble; and there had been no communication with Chatto since leaving the Plate.

If only he could have a drink. But as matters stood, he was broke and he was not going to risk another excursion into the first-class cabins. He suffered, mentally and physically. On occasion he feared that he might be on the brink of madness; he fought back, tried to subdue his obsession with Chatto and his own disastrous fall.

Tom's weather sense told him that the real blow was not far off. The wind, the roaring westerlies that blew around the pitch of the Horn almost without cease, was coming up to full strength and conditions would be bad off the great bleak cape that marked the southern extremity of the South American continent. Fullbright remained on the bridge throughout the day as his command neared Cape San Juan on Isla de los Estados, with some two hundred miles yet to go to Cape Horn.

He consulted frequently with Tom Chatto, discussing the tactics that were open to him. The steamships were, of course, better placed for the passage than were the windjammers: the westerlies, blowing sometimes up to a hundred knots, did not force steamships back to await a better opportunity of fighting into a shift of wind that would carry them on farther. But high seas still had their problems; off the pitch of the Horn, the biggest ship was little more than a cork to be tossed about at the sea's whim.

'I shall hold to the north, Mr Chatto.'

'You've the southern ice in mind, sir?'

Fullbright nodded as they pored over the chart. 'Yes. Any drift could be dangerous. I prefer to hold away—always did when the weather really blew up.'

Tom said, 'We'll have to stand clear of the Diego Ramirez, sir.'

'I know that, Mr Chatto. I'll move to a more southerly track as appropriate, you may be sure.'

Fullbright received reports from the other deck officers. Extra strops had been sent to the anchors and cables, all boats' falls had been overhauled and the tautness of the gripes checked. Likewise the funnel stays, the standing and running rigging on the fore- and mainmasts. The guardrails had been checked throughout the ship, lifelines had been rigged where appropriate, the pianos and other heavy furniture in the lounges had been secured for bad weather, and in the chief steward's stores and pantries and galleys everything movable had, so far as possible, been clamped down hard. The chief steward's eye had been on his glassware and crockery. Too many breakages and his end-of-voyage bonus might go for a burton. There was not much to prepare for in the purser's office other than to secure the typewriters—and stand by for the complaints about the motion, the cold and wet and anything else they could dream up, as though the ship's officers could wave a lordly hand and tell the weather what to do.

A discordant note came that evening from the engine room: there was trouble with some of the bearings of the main shafts, which were overheating. Harrison asked the bridge for permission to reduce the revolutions.

'Essential, Chief?' Tom asked.

'Yes.' Harrison's tone was uncompromising. Tom called the Captain, who had gone to his day cabin for a brief nap before the bridge would need him for a virtual full due. Fullbright spoke himself to Harrison, and grudgingly allowed the reduction in revolutions. With a warning.

'Depending on the weather, Chief, I may need full revolutions at short notice.'

'Understood,' Harrison said. 'I'll be doing my best.' He understood very well. Where windjammers could be dismasted, steamships could be broached-to, fall off the wind and lie broadside to massive waves that could, and very often did, pound the

185

vessel to pieces as she lay helpless, at the mercy of those seas, trying unavailingly to fight her head back into the wind and bring the sea ahead rather than so dangerously on the beam. And to prevent this happening, full revolutions could be needed very quickly indeed.

A sense of unease had begun to be noticeable among the passengers, as though they knew that the engines were not working at full efficiency. Ainsworth noted this unease, deducing it largely from the querulousness of those who came to the office with questions, silly questions some of them, but not all. They wanted reassurance. Ainsworth went to the bridge for a word with the Captain. Passenger reassurance was important, it was what they paid for.

'What do you suggest?' Fullbright asked.

'Your table in the saloon, sir. Anything you say would soon get round.'

'You're suggesting I dine there tonight?'

'Yes, sir.'

'I thought you might be,' Fullbright said with a sigh of exasperation. This was no time to be addled by questions from passengers, but Ainsworth was right.

The very presence of the Captain in the saloon was itself reassurance. Everything must be all right if the Captain wasn't on the bridge—steering the ship, as the less aware of the passengers tended to think he did. No emergencies if the Captain could spare the time to eat. 'All right, Ainsworth, no promises but I'll be there if at all possible.'

Ainsworth grinned. He knew the Old Man's thoughts. 'Up to God, sir?'

Fullbright gave a brief laugh. 'Up to God, Purser. But then, isn't everything?'

ELEVEN

Indeed everything was up to God, and that included in a very positive and present sense the safety of ships at sea. But that night God permitted and Fullbright attended dinner, with his steward standing in his usual place behind his chair.

The men stood as he joined them. 'Please sit down, gentlemen,' he said. The ship was lurching quite heavily; plates slid on the starched white tablecloth and

187

were brought up by the fiddleys. Some soup was spilled. The men were easy enough, showing rather elaborately that they weren't worried by bad weather, even those who hadn't travelled before. The women were not so reticent; Fullbright noted with relief that Lady Moyra was not present. He was always thankful for small mercies, though in all conscience there was nothing small about Lady Moyra other than her mind.

A spinster, a Miss Turner-White, started the ball rolling. 'Have you come from the bridge, Captain Fullbright?'

Apart from the time taken to shift into mess dress, the answer was yes. 'I have, Miss Turner-White.'

'It's so *very* windy.'

'Breezy certainly—'

'I found it quite impossible to go out on deck.'

Then stay inside, Fullbright thought ungraciously. Aloud he said, 'I'm sorry, Miss Turner-White. It's often like that, you know, in the High South latitudes. At present we're in the Roaring Forties.'

'Oh dear,' Miss Turner-White said faintly. Fullbright had noted soon after sailing day from Liverpool that she too was in her forties, if not more, though far from roaring. 'I don't like the sound of that, Captain Fullbright.'

Foot in it straight away. Fullbright calmed the waters. 'It's nothing to worry about. It's just a nautical term, a name, that's all.'

'They don't *roar*,' the man opposite Miss Turner-White said, and gave a high-pitched laugh, more of a girlish giggle, Fullbright thought, having heard it before.

Miss Turner-White flushed. But she persisted. 'Is there any danger, do you think, Captain Fullbright?'

'No, there's not. The passage of Cape Horn will be uncomfortable probably, but as for danger, no. You're in good hands, Miss Turner-White, I assure you—'

'Oh, dear. I *most certainly* didn't mean to suggest anything to the contrary, Captain Fullbright...'

'I realize that. But really, you mustn't worry. Ships have been rounding Cape Horn for a very long time. All of us—the ship's officers, and most of the deck crew—have been round in sail more times than you could count.' Fullbright put on a jovial, old-salt act. 'Barnacles, that's what we are. Shellbacks who've spent their lives at sea. Come wind or weather, Miss Turner-White...' He knew he was waffling; the spinster lady somehow had that effect on him. But he believed he had convinced her, and hoped the word would spread that they weren't on the point of sinking. But the possible effect of anything he had said was somewhat negated by what happened as the main course was served. The head waiter came into the saloon and spoke to Fullbright's steward, who bent and said into Fullbright's ear, 'Wanted on the bridge, sir.'

Fullbright nodded, laid his napkin on the table, and excused himself. 'Work,' he said briefly, and walked through the saloon followed by his steward. There was no passenger who failed to see his departure and to speculate upon it. Coming down at all had perhaps been a mistake. 'What is it, Mr—'

'Lifeboat, sir. Two points on the port bow, about six cables distant.'

Fullbright brought up his binoculars, picked up the bearing. The visibility was poor, the air filled with spindrift and darkness was coming down fast. But he made out men in the boat, some of them lying across their oars, others seemingly collapsed on the boat's bottom-boards or half across the thwarts.

'Bring her round to port, Mr Forster.' The Chief Officer had been on the bridge when the sighting was made and had taken over pending the Captain's arrival. 'We'll give her a lee.'

'You'll pick them up, sir?'

'What else, Mr Forster?'

Forster sucked his teeth; the conditions were far from good. There were dangers in rescue. The *Orvega's* bows swung to port under starboard wheel. Fullbright, still with his binoculars on the lifeboat, said, 'They'll be in bad shape.' He called to the bridge messenger. 'Get below, lad, warn the doctor and the chief steward.' Turning to the Chief Officer he said, 'Below, Mr Forster, and stand by with the hands in the fore well-deck, port side. I'll take over the bridge.'

As Forster went down the ladder, Fullbright brought the ship across the wind, keeping the liner's bulk between it and the lifeboat. With the force of the gale removed as the liner closed, the boat rode a little easier as she came into the *Orvega's* lee. Fullbright went to the engine-room telegraph and wrenched the handles over to Standby. Then he spoke directly to Harrison via the voicepipe and briefly gave him the facts.

'Just keep her moving gently ahead, Chief. I'll be ringing down for stop presently.'

He moved into the port wing of the bridge and stared down as the liner drifted up towards the lifeboat. He fancied all the men were dead.

The reduced speed was noted in the saloon. Tom Chatto excused himself from his table and went out on to the open deck. He saw the lifeboat, and went fast for the fore well-deck. He found Forster taking charge, together with the bosun who had a heaving line ready to cast as soon as the ship closed in further. Forster was reaching the same conclusion as the Captain. 'All corpses by the look of it.'

Tom was inclined to agree; but the boat had to be investigated nevertheless. Forster, gauging the distance, called out, 'Right, bosun!'

The bosun cast the heaving line. His aim was good; the monkey's fist at the end of the thin codline caught round a thwart and held fast. There was no movement in the boat. Forster leaned over the guardrail and called out, 'Below there! Take the line for God's sake, there's no time to waste.' In the well-deck hands were standing by with a heavier line, the inboard end of the heaving line already secured to its eye.

No response. Forster swore roundly. Tom, watching for any sign of life, believed he saw a hand move. Forster didn't believe him. A moment later Tom was certain. The hand swayed over one of the thwarts, as though reaching blindly for an oar.

Tom said, 'They need someone down there, sir. Someone to make fast.' The liner was moving closer; then a scend of the sea lifted the boat and cast her hard against the great steel side of the *Orvega*. There was a crunching sound, the sound of breaking woodwork. There was no time to lose now. Disregarding the Chief Officer, Tom called to the bosun to get the heavier rope over the side pronto. When the order had been carried out, Tom climbed the guardrail, lowered himself down the liner's side and got a grip on the rope with hands and feet. He went down like a monkey.

The boat rose on a wave to meet him, then fell away again. He waited until the next rise, then dropped into the sternsheets. Making his way dangerously along the boat while keeping a grip on the rope that held him to the ship, he made the line fast to the staghorn in the bows. Swaying as the lifeboat lifted and fell and banged against the ship's side, he yelled up at the well-deck that for the time being the boat was secure but was in danger of breaking up should there be more impact against the ship's side. The occupants, dead or alive, could perhaps be lifted out singly but Tom believed the best and fastest course would be to swing out the liner's derrick and bring the lifeboat bodily inboard. It appeared that Fullbright thought the same. As Tom stood by in the boat, the hands began swinging out the derrick with lines and strops attached to the hook at the end of the whip.

As the derrick was swung out to port and the whip went down, the guardrails were removed from the section above the lifeboat. Tom stood by below to take the strops at the ends of the lines. Working as fast as he could, stumbling with the boat's heave over the spread bodies, he ran the strops beneath the lifeboat fore and aft, and led the eyes to the hook of the derrick.

He cupped his hands to the deck far above. *'Hoist away!'* As the strain came on the whip and then on the lifeboat's frames, Tom held on tight. There was a lurch and a swaying motion as the lift began. As Tom came a little above deck level, the derrick was swung inboard and then lowered away until the lifeboat with its grim cargo was resting on the liner's number-one cargo hatch.

Forster's face was sour: Tom had taken the initiative; Forster would not forget that he had been shown up before the bosun and the hands by a newly-joined Second Officer. And before the Captain as well.

The doctor had been waiting with Sister Moloney for the boat to be brought inboard. As soon as it was in a safe position Murphy got on with the job. Fullbright and Forster had been nearly right: of fifteen men aboard, thirteen were dead. The two survivors were suffering from exposure to extreme cold and wet, and near-starvation. An examination of the lifeboat, as Fullbright put the ship back on her course and rang down for full away on the engines, showed that the emergency food stowage was empty as were the freshwater barricoes. There was no sign of any flares such as Verey lights, or even of matches in waterproofed boxes. The name on the lifeboat's bows was *Falls of Dochart*. Tom knew the ship by reputation: a windjammer, a fast sailer engaged in the Australian wool trade.

The two seamen were taken below to the sickbay. 'It'll be a slow recovery,' Murphy reported to the Captain on the bridge. 'I'll let you know when they're fit to be questioned, sir.'

Fullbright nodded. 'Thank you, Doctor. You have hopes, then, for their recovery?'

Murphy had; there were no physical injuries to the survivors, although blood had soaked into the clothing of some of the dead, and some had broken limbs. As Murphy went back below, Fullbright turned to Tom.

'Well done,' he said. 'You showed good seamanship—and quick thought. Not that I'd have expected less of my officers.' That was all; no criticism of the Chief Officer's apparent dithering. Fullbright went on, 'You know what we have to look out for now, Chatto?'

'A windjammer, abandoned and in a bad way, sir. Probably dismasted...or with stove-in hatches and flooded holds.'

'And currently a danger to other shipping, if she's still afloat,' Fullbright said. 'We'll sharpen the lookout from now on, and if we come upon her...well, that's when we decide what to do.'

Next morning, in daylight, the dead men were sewn into canvas shrouds and once more Captain Fullbright read the committal service as they went overboard into the cold, grey, heaving seas, the lonely and desolate seas at the world's bottom. Their boat would remain lashed down to the fore hatch for discharge at Valparaiso, where it would be required as evidence at the inquiry that would be held into an apparent wreck.

After the service Tom was buttonholed by Grace Handley. 'Quite the hero,' she said, smiling. 'You don't mind my congratulating you, do you?'

'Good heavens, it was nothing much. just doing the job. Anyone else would have done the same.'

'But anyone else didn't. Or so I hear.'

Tom got the drift. The passengers would have been talking, and a crowd of them had in fact been watching from the for'ard walkway joining the two sides of the promenade deck below the Captain's deck. He said, 'Don't listen to gossip, Grace. And for God's sake don't involve me in it.'

For her part she got his drift as well. She said, 'Well, I won't criticize loyalty.' She flushed, realizing the import of what she'd said: loyalty to her husband was perhaps a different kettle of fish... She covered up, saying, 'You're going to be a celebrity whether you like it or not—'

'Well, I won't like it,' he said roughly. 'All those men lost...I wonder if passengers ever bother to think about—about that sort of thing. Men dying to carry them across the seas. And doing it for a starvation wage, very often in a ship that should never be allowed out of port. Coffin ships, we call them. Not that that applies to the *Falls of Dochart*. She was a fine ship.'

He turned away and left her looking after him quizzically.

Next day Murphy reported the two survivors fit enough to answer questions. Questions were very necessary; Fullbright needed to know, in advance of any sighting, what condition of wreck was adrift in the danger area of Cape Horn.

The two were deckhands. Their ship,

bound from the Cape of Good Hope to Melbourne for wool and carrying an outward cargo of bagged rice, had been trying day after day, week after week, to drive into those tearing westerlies, waiting for that elusive shift of wind that would carry them round the Horn into the less tricky waters of the South Pacific and the Southern Ocean. Then, instead of that shift, they had been struck by an exceptionally heavy squall that the vessel's Master had estimated to be blowing at well over a hundred knots. That sudden vicious blow, accompanied by high seas that had swept the deck from stem to stern, had breached the covers of the fore hatch, and had risen above the level of the half-deck where the apprentices lived, had proved too much for the foremast, the only mast then carrying sail, and it had gone in a splintering of woodwork and a crack like thunder from the canvas of the fore upper tops'l and mains'l. Three hands had been swept overboard with not the faintest chance of rescue; and in its fall the foremast had brought down the bare poles of the main upper topmast. The vessel had fallen off the wind and had lain helpless, and the gale and sea between them, as she rose to the wave-crests, had taken out the mizzenmast like a broken stick.

'The Old Man passed the order to abandon,' the seaman said. This was to Sister Moloney, before the Captain came below. 'Some of the 'ands, they got lost when the boat was lowered.'

'And the Old Man?'

'Stayed aboard. Sort of thing he would do, mad as a bleedin' hatter. Said the good Lord would see to him. I dunno...didn't see to some of us, did He?'

'He saw to you,' Sister Moloney pointed out gently. 'Did he remain aboard alone, or—'

'God, Sister, or the Old Man?'

Sister Moloney said primly, 'Don't be cheeky—or sacrilegious either.' Then she smiled; if the man could make silly jokes, he wasn't doing too badly. He answered her question. The steward, he referred to him as the peggy, had stayed along with two of the young apprentices; they had disobeyed the order to leave in the lifeboat—bloody idiots they were, in the man's opinion. He said he didn't know if God had stayed, but likely enough He had: the Old Man was a bit of a Bible-basher. Or had been; he was most probably dead by now, along with the others. And dead heroes were no use to anyone.

The extra lookout demanded by Fullbright was maintained with vigilance. It was not impossible that the men still aboard the windjammer lived yet; a battered hulk could remain afloat for a long time, and the Master's accommodation aft could still be habitable. On the other hand, of course, the fact of the broken hatch-covers, admitting seawater, could drag the ship down so that she would ride waterlogged, soggy, upper deck awash, just below the surface, to be a danger to other shipping on passage of the Horn. Tom Chatto's thoughts went back continually to the old *Pass of Drumochter*, and to Captain Landon. Landon would have acted in the same way as the *Falls of Dochart's* Master: he would never have left his ship under any circumstances. The ship had been his home and possibly the same was the case aboard the wrecked ship. Tom knew too that he himself would have stayed aboard. Or he hoped he would have done. One never really knew what one's reactions would be until one was faced with the particular situation that demanded one's all.

Off watch, Tom found that Grace Handley's prediction was correct. He came in for many congratulations from the passengers, particularly those at his own table in the saloon, until he made it plain that the subject would be better dropped. The widow Westby's daughter had bombarded him with what he regarded as sheep's eyes, or the devotion of a spaniel; and this he had found embarrassing. However, she only looked and didn't utter; she was as silent as the departed Mrs Tidy. Bolsover had made much of it, hinting that Tom's conduct would go down well with the Pontarena family. Thus reminded, Tom became aware that he hadn't spared much thought recently for Dolores. This gave him something to ponder. Possibly his feelings were not all that deep.

Also, he hadn't given much thought to Patience. But now that he did, he knew that Patience wouldn't be giving up easily.

It was only two days after the pick-up of the lifeboat that the masthead lookout reported a sighting of a windjammer that appeared to be in much trouble, almost mastless and drifting with the wind and sea. Fullbright was called immediately to the bridge. The vessel was dead ahead and about two miles distant in the still poor visibility. Fullbright stared through his binoculars. This had to be the *Falls of Dochart:* she would have been driven east by the force of the westerlies, driven from her abandoning position to lie well easterly of Cape Horn.

Fullbright called the Chief and First Officers to the bridge. The sighting had been made in Tom's watch, thus he was part of the conference. The danger to shipping was obvious; in the prevailing weather conditions, in the much reduced visibility, a windjammer, or even a steamship, could plough into the vessel and do herself considerable damage.

'It's up to us,' Fullbright said. 'I propose to pass a tow and take her out of the shipping lanes.'

Forster gaped. 'In this weather, sir?'

'In this weather, Mr Forster.'

'But...where will you take her, sir? Not, surely, all the way to Valparaiso?'

'I see no reason why not, Mr Forster. Once the tow's passed—that'll be the tricky part, of course—there's no reason why she shouldn't be taken anywhere. But depending how things go, I may decide to take her into Puerto Montt. However, we shall see. For now, Mr Forster, I'll ask you to prepare to tow aft. You know the drill—seaboat to stand by on the quarter, ready to take a grass line across to the windjammer. If there's no one left aboard, and I'll be finding that out shortly, I'll need to put hands aboard to secure the towing pendant inboard of the windjammer. And of course there'll be an officer in charge of the seaboat.' Fullbright looked Tom in the eye. 'Well now, Mr Chatto. How do you fancy the job?'

Tom was honest. He said, 'Not much, sir. But I think I can cope.'

'I'm quite sure you can or I wouldn't have asked you. Very well, Mr Chatto, get below and prepare yourself. You may have to remain aboard to take charge, so take plenty of appropriate clothing and so on. When you're ready, report back to the bridge for your final orders.'

Tom left the bridge. Sail again, he thought, and I'd believed I'd done with it for good. He was thinking it only too likely that he would have to remain aboard with a few hands to tend the tow. Well, he would manage; he'd been First Mate in sail, and he still knew the ropes. He went to his cabin and stuffed warm clothing into a canvas kitbag, his feelings mixed. There was going to be danger; but there was an element of sheer excitement as well, and anticipation. The wreck wouldn't be much of a command, but it might well be his first if the Master of the *Falls of Dochart* had died.

TWELVE

Fullbright had given a blast on the steam siren and then used his megaphone to call up the semi-derelict vessel. To his astonishment, a man was seen to emerge from the after saloon ladder on to the poop. A hand waved in acknowledgment of Fullbright's shout. The liner was now some three cables off the windjammer and the damage could be seen clearly. Fullbright, who had stopped engines, now went to Slow Ahead to manoeuvre his ship closer and stand between the windjammer and the westerlies. This done, his amplified voice carried down on to the sailing ship's poop.

'I've picked up your lifeboat,' he called, 'and I can see the damage for myself. Can you hear me?'

There was an answering wave. Fullbright saw that the man was young, little more than a boy—an apprentice, obviously. The Master might or might not be still alive. Fullbright called again. 'I intend to pass a tow and take you in charge. Understood?'

There was another wave.

'Right! Stand by for my seaboat. I'll be putting an officer aboard you.'

Fullbright lowered the megaphone and nodded at the Chief Officer, who left the bridge. A moment later Tom reported back. 'All set?' Fullbright asked.

'All set, sir.'

'Good.' Fullbright reached out, gave Tom's hand a firm shake. 'The best of luck, young Chatto. It's not going to be easy. The sea never is, especially in this benighted spot! Just do your best.'

Tom made his way aft, down to the steerage decks from where the tow would be passed through the fairleads from the bitts on either side of the stern. As he went down through the first- and second-class decks, the seaboat was lowered on the falls to drift astern, ready to take the eye of the grass line, which in due course would be backed up by the heavy towing pendant.

Bolsover and Tidy were watching from the aftermost part of the boat deck. Grace Handley was with them, not from choice but because, talking together, they happened to come up alongside her as she looked down at the stern.

'Of course, there'll be salvage,' Bolsover, ever knowledgeable, remarked. 'A good, fat sum, I shouldn't wonder! If they get her into harbour, that is.'

Tidy nodded. 'Like prize money, in wartime?'

'That's right. Most goes to the Master and officers. Our Mr Chatto should do well out of it.'

'That,' Tidy said, 'is what motivates them, I suppose. Money, it's always the same. Do anything for money, some will. Same in the Army...Indian Army, they got more pay which is why the officers chose it. Not a sense of duty, *or* love of bloody India...beg pardon, Mrs Handley, didn't see you.' He gave her an ingratiating smile. 'What do you think?'

'I think you should stop being so bloody commercial,' she snapped, and walked away for'ard. Tidy and Bolsover exchanged sardonic looks.

'Put your foot in it, chum,' Bolsover said, and winked.

Down aft, Patience watched the preparations for the tow. He had picked up from the men tending the grass line that Chatto was being sent away in charge. He sucked his teeth, went on watching as the heavy line was sent through the fairleads, its eye dipping down towards the seaboat now lying beneath the ship's counter. The engines were stopped now; the liner lifted and fell to the heave of the sea, the seaboat itself rose and fell alarmingly, sometimes lifting almost to impact against the stern's overhang.

No easy job for someone Patience still thought of as a greenhorn when compared with his own long experience of sail. No easy job even to get down into the seaboat and take it across the gale-driven water, let alone make the tow fast at the other end and then take charge of what looked like a very waterlogged sailing ship, a ship at what looked like her last gasp.

Maybe Chatto would make a bird's nest of the job, maybe kill himself in the process. Towing was always tricky, and in the prevailing conditions it could be suicide. Patience had had experience of towing, both from the viewpoint of the towing ship and that of the ship under tow. He knew the dangers. For one thing, tows could part; if the towing pendant—a heavy rope with a wire halfway along its length to act as a spring-lifted, the whole point being that the wire kept it beneath the water, then the tow became bar-taut and all manner of nasty things could happen when it parted under heavy stress.

Something stirred in Patience's mind. That obsession of his...and remembrances of the past, of days when he had hopes of a command in sail. He was still in possession of his Master's Certificate in sail, they hadn't taken that away from him—they couldn't, for there had never been anything impugned against his ability, against his seamanship. He was still a seaman at heart; there was so much to be regretted, things that could never be put right.

What the hell.

He turned away from the rail. As he

turned, he came face to face with Tom Chatto. They stared for a moment at each other. Then on a sudden impulse Patience reached out and put a hand on Tom's shoulder.

'Good luck, boy,' he said, and turned again, and went off rather shamblingly to his shared cabin.

Tom had been taken flat aback. He gave no response, but shrugged and returned to the job in hand. When the inboard end of the grass line had been secured to the bitts, and the heaving line attached to its eye had been made fast, the line was grappled in by the boat's crew. The heaving line would be the first to go aboard the windjammer, either taken by one of the men still aboard or by Tom, who would have to find a way of clambering up on to the deck. Behind the line would come the grass line, ready now to be paid out into the water and be hauled along behind the seaboat. The weight would be no problem; grass lines floated, took their own weight. But it would be heavy enough to heave aboard the windjammer. With no powered windlass available, it would be a case of sweat and beef, pulley-hauley by manpower, and not many men to do it.

Buffeted by the wind, wet through already from the waves and swirling spindrift, Tom went over the after guardrail, gripping the grass line with frozen hands and seabooted feet. In the sailing warships of Queen Victoria's Navy, the seamen had found ropes easier to climb with bare feet. But Tom doubted if they'd ever done that in the High South latitudes.

His feet took one of the thwarts in the seaboat, and hands grabbed him in safely.

One of the men shouted something, pointed upwards.

Tom looked up.

Patience was swarming down the grass line.

There had been no time for argument; Tom had told Patience to get back up. Patience was a passenger, not a member of the crew. He had no right and he wasn't needed. Patience was adamant: it was too late now, he was there and he was going to stay. Tom had to let it go; seamen didn't mess about in boats in a seaway. Already they had drifted clear of the liner and Tom had to take charge without more delay.

'Give way together,' he ordered. Patience

crouched in the bow, being a hindrance to the oarsmen. Muscles responded to Tom's order as he took the tiller and brought the seaboat round, heading out across the turbulence, making progress but making it cruelly slowly as the waves lifted the boat, tossing it like a cork, bringing the oars clear of the water so that muscles strained at nothing, met no resistance so that the half-frozen men, their feet braced against the stretchers, fell back on those behind them.

No time to worry about Patience and his possible motive. If he was there to make trouble...but surely that wouldn't be the case. Not in a situation like this. Trouble would risk the man's own skin.

Almost everyone aboard the liner was watching the progress of the seaboat. Off-watch firemen and trimmers had come up from the depths of the ship; off-duty stewards mingled with them. From the bridge, as the ship began to take on a list to starboard from the sheer weight of sightseers, the Captain sent down orders for the deck officers to disperse them. The officers had their work cut out at the start, but crisp orders that allowed no argument had their due effect. Forster, gone aft now to supervise the tow, muttered away to himself, muttered about suicidal missions and what was the Captain thinking about. And to send Chatto away in charge! Of all things, that was lunacy.

Chatto simply hadn't the experience. Forster himself had, but he hadn't pressed the point and neither had Fullbright. That could be for either of two reasons: Fullbright needed his Chief Officer aboard; or he didn't believe him capable of doing the job. Forster clung to the first alternative, allowed the other to slide away with the tearing wind.

He'd been there when Patience, suddenly emerging from the after screen with an almost mad look on his face, had made a dive for the rail and the grass line and gone down into the boat. Forster, taken totally by surprise as much as Chatto had been, had failed to stop him. Now he asked the bosun who the man was.

'Steerage passenger, sir. One the master-at-arms found in the first class, before Buenos Aires that was. Name of Sivyer, sir.'

'Really. What the bloody hell's he doing?'

'Dunno, sir.' The bosun paused. 'I've spoken to him once or twice...seemed to know the sea. I reckon he was a seaman, likely enough in sail.'

'No excuse for interfering with the ship's business.'

'No, sir. But I'd say it shows guts.'

Forster fumed. A report would be made to the Captain. Passengers, whether qualified seamen or not, had to be kept in their places. At sea, they didn't rate with a tinker's cuss. Even Fullbright, if ever he found himself a passenger in another Captain's command, would have to keep his trap shut...

Tidy and Bolsover had also seen Patience embark; they were as astonished as anyone.

'What's he up to?' Tidy wondered.

Bolsover couldn't answer that one. He remembered the various conversations they'd had, boozing in Tidy's cabin. Sivyer even then had been something of an enigma, never revealing much about himself, but he'd undoubtedly exhibited curiosity about young Chatto. Both Bolsover and Tidy saw something fishy, but had no idea what it could be. Later, after the Captain's order had driven them from their grandstand view, they tried to pump Grace Handley. Chatto might have spoken to her about Sivyer. But Grace rounded on Bolsover, told him tartly to mind his own business.

'Now you've put *your* foot in it,' Tidy said when she'd left them.

'And bollocks to you too. What about a drink?'

Tidy was always willing.

The seaboat had reached the windjammer now. There was a man on her deck, a youth who looked like an apprentice. Tom shouted up to him as the seaboat surged up and down, held off the ship's side by the crew, using their oars now as bearing-out spars.

'Stand by for a heaving line!'

The youth lifted a hand in acknowledgment. It was Patience who cast the heaving line, well and truly aimed. His skills were there still, despite the wasted years of despair. He was back in his element. The apprentice caught the line neatly and began to heave in. As the eye rose from the water, Patience leapt dangerously for the windjammer's side, got a grip on a projection in the hull, hung for a moment getting his breath back, then heaved himself up to lie on the bulwarks before dropping down inboard. He called down to the seaboat. 'Now you, *Mister* Chatto. It's going to take a lot of pull.'

Tom did as Patience had done, damaging a hand on the iron projection in the process. Blood ran unnoticed: damage had to be accepted aboard a windjammer. Finding his feet after he had negotiated the bulwarks, he joined Patience and the apprentice, heaving the grass line up the side and then leading the eye back through the bullring in the bows and dropping it over the bitts on the fo'c's'le-head. It was a heavy job and it took time. All of them, despite the exertion, felt freezing cold in the bitter wind that plucked at them and blew through their supposedly weatherproof clothing without cease. Tom noted that Patience, in fact, had, apart from a lifejacket, nothing beyond his pea jacket; but it was his own business if he froze to death. The tow passed, Tom went to the side and shouted down to the boat's crew. Four extra hands had been sent, to be used aboard the windjammer.

'You men as detailed. Come aboard now. Cox'n?'

'Yes, sir?'

'Carry on back to the ship. Report the tow secured inboard of the windjammer.'

There was an answering wave and the seaboat, lurching heavily, turned away for the *Orvega*. Patience, watching it make its difficult progress, spoke to Tom. 'You'll need a thorough inspection, soon as possible.'

'I know that, Mr Patience.' Tom took a deep breath: there was something to be put straight right from the start, put straight very firmly and without holding back. 'I'll be grateful for your advice, Mr Patience, make no mistake about that. But you're a passenger aboard the *Orvega*...you have no authority here. It's to be understood that I'm in charge.'

Their eyes met. Patience's look was difficult to interpret. He said, 'You may be jumping the gun, Mr Chatto. The lad told me when I got aboard...the Captain's still alive.'

The 'lad' referred to by Patience was the senior apprentice, by name Jack Maynard. Tom had a word with him: Captain Lee was certainly still alive but only just. He had injured a leg when the ship had been dismasted, and the leg was poisoned, Maynard believed. The other apprentice who had remained behind, disobeying the Master's order, had subsequently been lost overboard. Now there were just the two left, Maynard and a sick Master. Maynard gave Tom a summary of the damage. Apart from the dismasting, there was the cargo, partially flooded as a result of the fore hatch-covers being stove in. The after hatches were so far intact; but the cargo was bagged rice, and rice swelled when the sea got into it. Maynard and his fellow apprentice had manhandled as many bags as they could manage out of the fore hold to be jettisoned overboard, and for the time being the danger had been contained. As for the rest of the ship, the half-deck house had gone, smashed to splinters, the wheel had been taken out of the poop as though it had never existed at all, and the tween-decks were a shambles of shattered woodwork and twisted metal. But the ship lived on. Tom and Patience made a quick inspection for themselves. Patience was gloomy.

'We'll never make it,' he said, shaking his head as they came up from the tween-deck aft, by way of the ladder leading from outside the saloon and the officers' cabins. 'She's lying like a half-dead pregnant bloody duck...'

A voice, borne aft along the wind, shouted from for'ard: Maynard. 'Boat's reached the steamship, Mr Chatto. Hooking on to the falls now.'

Chatto went for'ard into the eyes of the ship to stand by the towing pendant. Any moment now, the *Orvega* would be taking up the strain.

Fullbright had spoken on the bridge to the Chief Engineer: much of the success or otherwise of the operation would depend on Harrison and his black gang, on the speed with which they put the orders into effect. It was going to be immensely tricky and would need a very fine judgment.

Forster remained aft, by the towing pendant. As Harrison went below to the starting platform, the report came by megaphone from the First Officer on the boat deck: 'Seaboat hooked on to the falls, sir!'

'Hoist away,' Fullbright called. As soon as the boat was reported at embarkation-deck level and the crew were out, Fullbright rang down for Slow Ahead on the engines and ordered the wheel five degrees to starboard. Below in the engine room, the Chief Engineer followed the orders as discussed on the bridge. Minimum revolutions until the strain of the tow had been taken up; then a very gradual increase. Harrison watched carefully, one eye on the telegraph repeater, an ear ready for the voicepipe from the bridge.

Once again, the passengers were out in force, thronging the open decks and never mind the weather. But this time they were well tended by the senior stewards, who ensured that the orders were obeyed and the sightseers as evenly distributed as possible. The interest had extended to Lady Moyra, watching, so far as she was able, from her stateroom port. Until the ship swung, that was, and the scene of activity vanished.

'Bother take it,' she said sourly to her maid. 'However, there we are, I suppose Captain Fullbright knows what he's doing but I'm sure I don't. Such a nuisance...the delay.'

'Yes, me lady.'

'People waiting in Valparaiso. I wouldn't have thought that wreck of a ship was worth it.'

'No, me lady.' What else could she do but agree? Lives were not half so important to the old besom as her own wants and comforts.

From the bridge Fullbright watched continually through his binoculars, staring aft as the tow began to lift and become taut under the strain. This was a critical moment. The towing pendant lifted, dripping water; then eased back. Fullbright gave a sigh of relief. If that pendant remained below the waves—for just so long as it did—they were safe. Safe from that worry, anyhow. There were the other worries: the cargo, the overall seaworthiness, the capacity of Chatto and the hands to cope with what they had found aboard the *Falls of Dochart*.

And the weather, as they moved westerly to come below Cape Horn.

For now, however, all was well. Fullbright saw the windjammer turn a little in response to the tow, and then settle into the liner's wake as the revolutions were gradually increased.

Captain Lee was in both senses the Old Man: like Landon had been, he was nearing seventy and would soon retire.

Or die; he appeared to Tom to have little time left. The poisoned leg was very bad, and the inflammation was spreading into his groin. Tom believed there was a strong likelihood of gangrene. Patience, who had found the statutory copy of *The Ship Captain's Medical Guide* in the saloon, said in a whisper, 'He's a goner, I suppose you realize that?'

Captain Lee, who was quite *compos mentis*, and whose hearing was evidently good, reacted quickly. 'I take issue with you, Mister Whoever-you-are—'

'Once First Mate in sail, Captain,' Patience said.

'That may be, but you are no medical man. I place my trust in God. I am not going to die. But I confess to being unable to fulfil my duties at this moment.' He gave a wince of pain, and tried to straighten his leg in his bunk. His hand shook a little as he brushed thick white hair from his eyes, very blue eyes in a face that showed pallor beneath the weatherbeaten surface. 'One of you must deputize...but remember this: while I live, I remain Master of the *Falls of Dochart*. Master...under God, you understand?'

'I understand, sir,' Tom said. He knew

222

well enough that Master under God was the formal Board of Trade designation of a shipmaster, used when the articles of agreement were opened at the start of every deepwater voyage. But there had been something much deeper than that in Lee's tone.

Outside the cabin, Patience said, 'We have a Holy Joe on our hands by the sound of it. But he'll not last long, you mark my words.'

Tom didn't comment. He went for'ard to where young Maynard was watching the tow. All seemed well; the *Falls of Dochart* moved ahead westerly. Slow, but it was progress to have picked up the tow successfully in the first place.

Seven crew all told, to tend a big disabled windjammer through the restless seas of the High South latitudes. It wasn't enough—of course it wasn't—but it simply had to be and that was all there was to it. Tom organized a system of watch-keeping, one in three, two men always on the fo'c'sle-head, the others resting unless the ship required them, which in fact it did: the off-watch periods would bring no rest until all the bags of rice, or anyway the greater part of them, were up from the fore hold and dumped overboard; and that was a back-breaking business as the heavy bags were hauled up the ladder to the deck. No derricks now; it had all to be done by hand, and mostly, as it turned out, without Patience's help. Patience wasn't exactly hanging back; but he was in no fit state for heavy physical work. The years ashore, the wasted years of bitterness, of poor eating, of too much drink, had done their debilitating work. He was less than half the man he'd been when First Mate of the *Pass of Drumochter*. There was no question now of his trying, or indeed wishing, to usurp Tom's authority. After that first day's work in the hold, Tom arranged that Patience should take most of the watch on the fo'c'sle and that Maynard should assist with the heavy work. Thereafter Patience sat on the bitts, holding fast to a lifeline, cocooned against the weather in clothing he'd found in one of the mates' cabins: an extra pea jacket, oilskin, woollen mittens, seaboots and sou'wester.

His vigil, largely a lonely one, gave him plenty of time in which to think. It was a curious experience, coming back again to sail, coming back to the vicinity of

Cape Horn, Cape Stiff as the shellbacks had known it, standing once again in the after accommodation, in the saloon and the Master's cabin, the Master's cabin that once could have been his. And being there, moreover, in company with young Chatto, now not so young, last seen as a snotty-nosed first-voyage apprentice. The jealousy that had consumed him ever since he'd embarked aboard the *Orvega* in Liverpool was beginning to give place to, or be overlaid by, something else. Patience didn't know quite what: a sympathetic understanding of the problems Chatto was taking on, even a grudging admiration for the way he was taking charge? Perhaps; Patience was a seaman still, and thought as a seaman. Young Chatto had knuckled under, metaphorically and literally cast aside his brassbound uniform and the comparative luxury of a steamship life, and was working his guts out as a deckhand.

Patience gave himself a little pat on the back, recalling once again that he himself had been Chatto's first seagoing mentor and instructor. One way and another, he hadn't done a bad job.

Time had to be spent in attending Captain

Lee. Tom took the duty upon himself. The old man was in much pain; using the medical guide, Tom did what he could. It wasn't much; the facilities were not there, not even hot water. The galley had gone, along with the half-deck house. No fires, no hot food. They all had to exist on the cold provisions in the tween-deck store which, though damaged by the rush of water along the tween-deck itself, had kept most of its stock intact in steel-lined bins and cupboards.

Tom had seen that creeping poison in the Captain's leg. It needed draining. Gritting his teeth, Tom used a knife he'd found in the remains of the galley, a butcher's knife. An incision brought some relief.

It was possible the doctor could be sent across from the *Orvega:* Tom mentioned this. Captain Lee would have none of it. 'I shall not risk more lives, Mister. That I shall not...I am an old man. Your great liner...there will be women and children aboard who may be in need of a medical man. The children especially...I would doubt your Captain would part with his doctor in any case. I commit myself to God, Mister. He will ordain...as He sees fit.' There followed a quotation from the Bible, somewhat long and rambling, Tom thought. Having quoted, Lee fell into an uneasy sleep and Tom went back on deck. The howling of the wind was like a sort of requiem, almost a leavetaking of an old mariner whose time had truly come.

No time to think of that now. The fore hold was not yet by any means cleared of its cargo. Tom, moving for'ard along the spray-swept deck with difficulty, leaning heavily into the wind, stopped to check the covers of the after hatch. They seemed to be holding. There was some relief in that.

'I've been thinking,' Patience said. Tom had joined him on the fo'c'sle; the tow was in good shape, though from time to time lifting briefly from the water as the windjammer's bows rose to a wave that rushed beneath to travel aft and then lift the stern. There was no chafing in the bullring and the eye was secure on the bitts. 'About the past. And the present. And God help me, the bloody future.'

Tom didn't comment; Patience was better left to expand in his own time. After a long pause, he did. 'I don't see any future. Except back at sea, and that doesn't look possible. Last time I was down in these waters...some difference, eh?'

'No good looking back,' Tom said. What else could he say? 'Look, if we come through this—'

'You'll put in a word, is that it, *Mister* Chatto?' There was a sardonic tinge; Patience was still Patience. 'A fat lot of good that'll do, and I'm not asking for it anyway. You've not had a quarter of my experience, boy. And I'm not crawling to you or anybody else.' There was another long silence, if silence was the word in the racket of the westerly gale. 'But the point is, being back here, well, it's made me take a look at things. Things I'd rather not have done. If you follow.'

'Conscience?'

'Call it that, yes. Not what you'd associate with me—that's what you're thinking. Right?' He didn't wait for an answer. 'I'd like to clear things up. Because I don't reckon we're going to come through this. You might say I've some confessions to make.' He gave a harsh laugh. 'Deathbed confessions, you might say.' Then, suddenly, he broke off. He was staring away to starboard, across the tumbling grey seas swept by the wicked greybeards of the roaring westerlies. Tom followed his gaze. Dimly through the foul visibility he saw a great, dark shape rearing from the water on a north-westerly bearing, jagged and menacing, a sight he recognized as quickly as Patience had done.

Captain Fullbright had announced his intention of holding well to the north, to avoid any drift down to the southern ice. He could scarcely have been closer: they were now off the pitch of the Horn. Deathbed confessions would have to wait.

From the liner's decks they had all seen the dim outline of Cape Horn. They were in the world's most treacherous area of storm and potential danger. Tidy was apprehensive; Bolsover reassured him.

'Ships have been coming round the Horn for centuries. Not all got lost.'

Tidy snorted. 'That's comforting, I don't think! What about those that did?'

'Tragedy,' Bolsover said solemnly. 'Ringing of the Lutine bell at Lloyd's. Lists of the dead.' He clapped the ex-soldier on the shoulder. 'You've seen action, out in India. You survived. Danger's in the mind, my friend.' He offered the customary panacea.

'Come below and have a drink.'

On the bridge Fullbright used his binoculars. He was familiar enough with Cape Horn. Almost an old friend, to be greeted at regular intervals, outward or homeward bound. No worries for an experienced master mariner—in steam, anyhow. Steam was a reassurance of its own. Provided nothing went wrong, of course. Surreptitiously Fullbright crossed his fingers in front of his body as he stood there in the starboard wing of the bridge.

In the moment that he did so, the voicepipe from the engine room whistled.

THIRTEEN

Harrison's voice was calm and controlled but there was urgency in it.

'Bearings running hot again, sir.'

'Now of all times. So?'

'I'll have to shut down. Soon as you give the word, sir. The sooner the better.'

'Damn it all, Chief, we're off the pitch of the Horn!'

'I know that. The engines don't. They've

230

spoken, they've bloody well shouted, and I can't ignore them.' Harrison paused, his tone altering as he went on, 'Permission to stop engines, sir? Otherwise they'll seize up.'

Fullbright said harshly, 'Very well, Chief. Stop engines. Make it as fast as possible—the repair.'

'You can be sure I'll do that, sir.' Harrison banged back the voicepipe cover angrily. Repair! Not quite the word. The bearings needed rest, that was it, and then a dockyard overhaul. Deck officers, sail-trained, were all the same: didn't understand a thing about machinery and believed the engines could move on indefinitely, all ready to obey the slightest whim of the bridge and obey it instantly. But engines were not like that at all. They were idiosyncratic, like people. They had personalities of their own, characteristics of their own. Bugger 'em... Harrison, as the telegraph pointer moved to Stop in confirmation of the Captain's verbal permission, passed the word to his Second Engineer. The engines died, the shafts stopped their spinning, the screws beneath the counter stopped in sympathy.

The vibration, so noticeable until now throughout the ship, also came to a stop.

It was an eerie experience; so much sudden silence. It was a frightening experience, too. With the ship evidently stopped, the most landlubberly person aboard could see the implications with Cape Horn looming off the starboard bow.

Lady Moyra didn't like it at all and complained to her maid. 'It's dangerous, Connolly. Someone ought to tell the Captain.'

Connolly, driven beyond her usual 'Yes, me lady', unable to stomach such unawareness, dared to say, 'I'm certain sure he must know, me lady.'

'Nonsense, how can you be sure? You simply don't know, do you?'

Rebellion died; Lady Moyra's tone had been belligerent, very down-putting. 'No, me lady.'

'There you are, then, I thought not. Go and tell someone the engine seems to have stopped and I think we should be told something. Not the Captain, perhaps. The purser. He will pass the message on. Off you go, Connolly. Quickly, girl.'

Almost in tears, Connolly left the

stateroom. Lady Moyra peered from her port. Cape Horn, if that was what she was looking at, seemed to be getting closer and who was going to stop them all crashing into it like an omnibus meeting a stone wall?

All deck officers were capable of communicating by semaphore. From the *Orvega's* bridge, the Officer of the Watch passed the Captain's message to the windjammer. Patience saw the waving arms in the wing of the bridge, and sent an acknowledgment: he had not lost that skill either. The message received, he called out to Tom, working in the fore hold.

'Engine-room breakdown,' Patience reported briefly, then gave his personal opinion of the black gang. 'So what do we do, eh? Reverse the roles, tow the liner?' He gave a jeering laugh. 'By God, that'd be the day. Talk of Liverpool, that'd be, when you got back! If you got back.'

Tom said, 'Joke over, Mr Patience. There's nothing we can do. You agree?'

Patience agreed. 'Nothing at all. Only stand clear if she drifts down on us. Come to think of it—we can't even do that.'

'We stand by to jump,' Tom said.

'They'll be able to send down a jumping ladder if they can't get a boat away. For a start, I'll get Captain Lee up on deck—we may not have much time.' He made his way aft, holding on to the lifelines. Patience kept a sharp eye on the liner, wallowing heavily in the waves, the spindrift flying over her decks on the wings of the westerlies.

Connolly was at the counter of the purser's office. She spoke to Ainsworth himself. 'Please, sir, my mistress says do you know the boat's stopped?'

Ainsworth stared in disbelief, then recognized that the girl was in a state of nerves and that there was no attempt at making a joke in poor taste. Lady Moyra was enough to get on anyone's wick and the girl was well and truly under her thumb. He said gently, 'Yes, I do know that, Miss Connolly.'

'And would you please tell the Captain, in case he doesn't know—'

'I assure you he knows,' Ainsworth said.

'But just in case.' Connolly stopped. Her face was flaming. 'Please, sir, it's not my idea...I know the Captain knows, but it's my job, sir—'

'I know. I'll make quite sure the Captain's told—you can tell Lady Moyra that.'

Connolly's face cleared a little. She almost curtsied. 'Oh, thank you, sir, thank you very much.'

When she had left the counter, one of Ainsworth's assistants asked, 'Shall I send the message to the bridge, sir?'

Ainsworth blew out a long breath: this young man was making his first voyage, but even so...'Don't you dare! Don't you bloody dare if you want to go on living. It may be our job to do whatever the passengers want. It may be our job not to tell blatant lies to them—but not to the extent of giving the Captain a heart attack.'

Fullbright paced the bridge, his anxieties mounting. He had no fear that he might be driven on to Cape Horn; the wind's force was pushing the liner easterly. The danger lay farther off than Cape Horn but was no less lethal: there might be a southerly drift, a drift that could take the ship down towards the southern ice, the great icefields of Antarctica. If that should happen, the future would scarcely bear thinking of.

They could drift for days, even weeks, finally to be brought to a stop by the ice and to find themselves locked into the frozen wastes, the hull eventually crushing beneath the weight of the frozen seas.

Then they would become yet another statistic, another loss to be registered at Lloyd's of London, a liner lost with upwards of twelve hundred souls.

If Harrison couldn't get his engines turning over again, there were few alternatives left. One of them would be to abandon before it was too late. But to do that, to attempt to get so many passengers into the boats in the prevailing weather conditions, would result in far too many casualties. It was an option that Fullbright would not consider, at least until there were vessels in the vicinity to pick up the survivors. Fullbright had not yet sent out distress calls by the ship's wireless; more information would be wanted from the engine room before ships on passage were alerted to a possible deviation from their courses. Also, the speed and direction of any southerly drift would have to be accurately assessed as it developed to prevent any rescue from deteriorating into a wild-goose chase in waters that could bring much danger to the Samaritans.

The other alternative was prayer. It so happened that on this voyage there was no clergyman in the passenger list. Any prayer would have to be organized and led by Fullbright himself. And public prayer could quickly lead to panic. For the moment, it was too dangerous. But Fullbright sent up a silent prayer of his own, glancing up as he did so at the two black spheres blowing from the starboard fore upper yardarm as a warning to any other shipping that his vessel was currently not under command.

The easterly drift continued. On the starboard bow, Cape Horn had already disappeared into the spray-filled distance. Fullbright climbed to monkey's island above the wheelhouse, looking aft at the tow and the *Falls of Dochart*. The windjammer, affected by the same drift, moved easterly with the liner. For the moment Fullbright saw no danger of collision; and there was no point in casting off the tow.

He thought of Chatto: that young officer had been landed with a bellyful of problems now.

In the engine room Harrison and his

engineers and greasers worked against time. They all knew the dangers well enough, knew just how many lives depended on their success. Reports were made as often as possible to the bridge. Harrison knew that Fullbright was not the man to keep bothering the starting platform with endless requests for information; and for that he was thankful.

'It's a dockyard job,' the Second Engineer said with a note of despair. 'A proper strip-down in Valparaiso. Or maybe Puerto Montt. They may have facilities.'

Harrison wiped his streaming face with a bunch of cotton-waste, streaking himself with oil. 'Got to get there first,' he said. 'I dunno... Look, there's only one thing I can see. Connect up one shaft. One shaft at a time, and rest the other. We'd make some sort of progress that way.'

'Bird with one wing, Chief. Not much cop.'

'Better than nothing. I'll put it to the skipper.' Harrison climbed the network of steel ladders, making for the bridge to talk directly to the Captain. Reaching the open deck, he was hit by the extreme cold, sharp contrast with the heat of the engine room. He shivered as a sea came almost level with the boat deck, drenching him with the spray blown from its crest. There were some compensations in being an engineer. Not many, though.

Like Fullbright, old Captain Lee saw prayer as the fitting, and only, response. He had been brought to the poop and had been lashed, wrapped in warm clothing, to a ringbolt in the deck. He was not bothered by exposure to the elements and, in spite of his reluctance to desert the old ship, he knew that Tom was right to have him handy by in case the windjammer had finally, and probably quickly, to be abandoned.

Tom joined him in prayer before going back for'ard to watch the tow and the drift of the liner. Lee prayed, conventionally enough, for the calming of the waters; a very relevant prayer in the prevailing conditions. 'I've known it work before now, Mister Chatto. Mind, I've taken care to lead a decent life, a clean life to the glory of God. That helps. Helps not only the good-living persons themselves. The analogy being that of the monks and nuns ashore, who atone by their way of life for the sinners. That is the theory. One day we shall all find out if it holds good.'

Tom believed the old man was going to find out quite soon. Leaving him to another prayer, he joined Patience on the fo'c'sle. The liner was maintaining her distance so far, and no further semaphore messages had come from Fullbright. Tom found himself pondering on what Lee had said about sinners and a decent life. Everyone was a sinner, some more than others, but Tom found that he was glad there had been no sin between Grace Handley and himself. Sin could perhaps act in a reverse sense to goodness and the clean life, rubbing off adversely on the non-sinners. In current circumstances, that would not be a good thing.

'There's a dockyard in Puerto Montt,' Fullbright said. 'I don't know what the engine-repair facilities might be, but presumably they can get assistance sent down from Valparaiso. From a ship-handling point of view, the entry's exceptionally tricky, but that's my worry.'

'So we use the one shaft at a time, sir?'

Fullbright nodded. 'Yes, I'll go along with you, Chief. I'll use the minimum revolutions needed to maintain safety. We'll nurse her along, see how far we can get. Any problems, keep me informed.'

Harrison went below. He reported up to the bridge when he reached the starting platform, and watched the telegraph pointer moving to Slow Ahead on the starboard engine. On the bridge, a semaphore message was sent across to the windjammer and within a couple of minutes strain came back on the towing pendant and the windjammer's bows swung in answer.

From now on there would be problems for Fullbright and the Officers of the Watch. The ship would be steaming on much reduced power and would be carrying a degree of opposite helm to compensate for the forward thrust being all on the one side, port and starboard alternately. But if all went well they would be held away from the dangers of the southern ice. There were other considerations, but not ones of a lethal character: a deviation in to Puerto Montt, and a possible disembarkation for onward transport overland to Valparaiso, would not be welcomed by the passengers. The purser would be in for a bad time.

He already was: the office had been

inundated with questions, though none so nonsensical as Lady Moyra's. When would the ship arrive at Valparaiso? Would those meeting the ship be informed of the delay? Would there be enough fresh provisions aboard to keep them fit if there was to be a long delay? How fast were they going now? Mostly unanswerable, but Ainsworth and his staff did their best. Normal routine was being adhered to, nothing must alarm the passengers. Service with a smile in the cabins and in the saloons. Utter misery along the steerage decks as the liner rolled and heaved, making slow progress westerly, coming back again to Cape Horn and its gloomy, frowning countenance, heading for what everyone hoped would be the easier waters of the South Pacific. No one had mentioned the Diego Ramirez rocks to the west of Cape Horn.

Aboard the *Falls of Dochart*, Captain Lee had been moved back to his cabin aft of the saloon: the prospect of having to abandon had receded once the message had come from Fullbright that way was to be resumed on one screw at a time. Tom Chatto, standing on the poop and looking aloft at what was left of the old windjammer's top hamper, heard the sound of singing from below. A hymn, in a quavering voice: *O God, our help in ages Past...* It was a moment of extreme poignancy, and one that Tom was never to forget throughout the years ahead. The voice faltered after a while; the singing stopped rather suddenly. Knowing what he might find, Tom went below to the cabin. The old man was lying, apparently peacefully, in his bunk, his eyes wide, a hand clutching his Bible. There was no movement, no sound. Tom bent, listening for a heartbeat, feeling for a pulse. There was nothing. Gently Tom drew the sheet over the white face.

Tom made a vow to himself as he looked down on death. Whatever happened now, he would bring the *Falls of Dochart* into safe harbour.

FOURTEEN

The weather worsened. It seemed scarcely credible, but it happened. The wind roared down upon the two vessels, battering and tearing at the liner's super-structure, tormenting the watch-keepers on the bridge. Fullbright remained, exposed to all the discomforts, watching out for other shipping, watching the windjammer astern, keeping an eye on the towing pendant which now began to rise, coming up bar-taut at intervals. All passengers were now forbidden the open decks; not that any of them had any desire to leave the enclosed spaces, though there was little comfort in the cabins or public rooms as the liner was thrown about like a cork. It was dangerous even to move along the alleyways with a hand on the guardrails that ran along the bulkheads. The main companionway outside the purser's office was lethal. Dr Murphy contended with a number of bruises, with sprained ankles, with several broken limbs that had to be set in plaster. Connolly sat in constant attendance upon Lady Moyra, who refused, wisely enough, to leave her bunk. In the first- and second-class saloons the stewards mostly stood about with starched napkins folded, unused, over their arms. In his storerooms, the chief steward shuddered at the occasional crash of crockery and moaned to the chef about the wicked waste of good food.

Once night came down it all seemed worse than ever.

'They don't know their luck,' Patience said. 'Lap of luxury and they don't realize it.' He paused, shivering as the continual spindrift lashed into his face. 'How do you fancy sail again? After the soft living in steam?'

'Not all that much. There are things I miss, but—'

'Like real seamanship? Like the sense of a job well done when you reach port after a filthy voyage? All your own effort. Not dependent on bloody engines, with all their stink and smoke?'

'Yes, I suppose so. What about you?'

Patience gave a harsh laugh. 'Why ask me? I'm washed up and I know it. Years ashore, years of hell. I'd give my back teeth for a berth aboard a windjammer again.'

'Not steam?'

'Not steam, boy, not steam.'

Tom's memory took him back to his first days aboard the *Pass of Drumochter*, when he'd been a first-voyage apprentice. He'd made a remark to Jim Wales, the senior apprentice, wondering why Patience, old to be a First Mate, had never opted for steam in order to advance his career. He recalled Wales's answer: Patience would just as soon drive a tram.

Now Tom asked, 'What are you going to do when we get to Valparaiso, Mr Patience?'

Patience jeered. 'You're still certain sure we're going to come through this, aren't you, boy?'

Tom nodded. 'Yes, I am.'

'Well, good on you! I hope you're right. Or do I? It'd be a good way to go—aboard a windjammer taking all that God can throw at us.' He paused again. 'Does that answer your question, *Mister* Chatto?'

'Perhaps. But if—when—we come through ...what then?'

'God knows,' Patience answered irritably. 'I don't.'

And there Tom left it. But he had a feeling that Patience might yet make a comeback. There was good in the man; he was no hanger-back in danger and he was still what he had been: a first-rate seaman. A report from Captain Fullbright in due course might not come amiss. But time would tell.

With the coming of darkness, Fullbright

could no longer see how the towing pendant was behaving. From time to time he checked the binnacle, keeping himself informed of how much extra helm was being needed to counteract the alternate port and starboard thrust of the single-screw propulsion. And wondered how long it would be before the Chief Engineer reported further trouble with the bearings. Bearings... Fullbright cursed the very existence of bearings that plagued a master mariner off the Horn. In the windjammers, if you lost a sail, you merely replaced it. Unless the masts had gone with it.

Pacing the bridge with difficulty, sliding downhill one moment and climbing a miniature mountain the next, Fullbright was conscious of a curious change of motion; or not quite that: it was more a kind of waggle, as of a duck's bottom. He called to the Officer of the Watch. 'Mr Norton, did you feel what I felt?'

'Yes, sir—'

'It's the tow. It's parted!' Fullbright moved fast for the engine-room telegraph and rang down Stop Engines, hoping that the slack of the tow would not foul his screws or rudder. Then he blew down the voicepipe. Harrison himself answered: like the Master, he was at his station in times of difficulty.

'Tow's parted, Chief. I'm going to stand by.' Fullbright snapped the cover back. Below, Harrison wondered, what next? Would Fullbright attempt the impossible, which was to take off Chatto and the others? A boat would never live in the sea that was running. To manoeuvre alongside with jumping ladders down could, just could, maybe, with luck, succeed; but could equally well result in the liner smashing into the windjammer and sending her under before there was a chance of bringing off any men.

Harrison wiped his hand across his forehead. Not his worry. And thank God for that! Whatever his opinion of the deck people, he did acknowledge that it was they who had to make the life-and-death decisions. Not him.

'It's parted, boy, it's bloody parted!'
The towing pendant had come up bar-taut after a monster greybeard had roared beneath the windjammer's hull from dead ahead, lifting her bow sharply skywards. Then it had slacked away. Now the

248

ship's head paid off to starboard and she began to come across the wind and sea, bringing the weather's force slap on to her broadside, the sort of situation that was every seaman's dread—that, and any prospect of being blown on to the rocks of a lee shore. Patience yelled into Tom's ear, cutting across the terrible racket of the wind. 'We'll broach-to, boy, can't avoid it now!'

Tom's breath was taken away by the wind. He knew Patience was right. They would lie helpless. He wondered what Fullbright would do once he realized the tow had parted. The liner was currently invisible in the filthy night, in the flying spindrift and the surging greybeards. Would she simply steam on, oblivious? Unlikely: the bridge watch-keepers would have felt the sudden lack of pull from aft, and anyway the men standing by the towing pendant in the after part of the ship would have seen it fall slack.

So would she ease her engines, and come back towards the struggling windjammer?

Patience believed she would. 'Let's pray she doesn't come too close,' he said, 'because if she does, there's nothing we can do about it.'

A sharp lookout was being kept aboard the liner as Fullbright, confirming Patience's belief, put his telegraph to slow astern. He intended to drop down on the helpless vessel and make an attempt to assess the situation—visually, if possible, through the night's blackness. In the roaring westerly it was doubtful if any megaphone-backed voice would carry across the sea. The likelihood of a sight was of itself doubtful, in fact; the semi-derelict vessel carried no navigation lights and the manoeuvre meant extreme danger for Chatto and the hands aboard the windjammer, but there was no other course: Fullbright could not merely steam ahead, leaving the vessel alone and without hope. But what could be the next move? Stand by to make a desperate attempt to bring the men off if she looked like foundering, then, if she remained afloat, continue standing by in the hope of a moderation in the weather making it possible to pass another tow?

The seafaring life was a case of making one decision after another, so often, as now, decisions that would mean someone's life or death.

A man could grow too old for that sort of thing.

Fullbright caught himself up short, gave himself a mental shake. To think like that was an indulgence, a dangerous one. He must never allow that.

There was a shrill whine from one of the many voicepipes on the bridge. The Officer of the Watch went fast for the one that connected with the after deck. He reported to the Captain: 'Chief Officer aft, sir, windjammer believed dead astern, and close.'

'Stop engines,' Fullbright ordered. 'Wheel twenty degrees to port.' He went himself to the engine-room voicepipe. 'Chief, we're coming down on her. Stand by to go ahead at a moment's notice—and connect up the second shaft. No time to worry about the bearings now.'

He snapped back the cover and moved fast into the starboard wing, then climbed to monkey's island. He brought up his binoculars. After half a minute he had picked up the darker blur of the struggling ship, a sight that disappeared and then came back again as she lifted to the crest of a wave, then once again vanished as she dropped down into the depths, the valley between one wave and the next.

He felt totally helpless. He could not approach too close; too dangerous for the men aboard the windjammer. The most he could do, perhaps, would be to give the vessel a lee by keeping his own ship between her and the wind and sea, a tricky business to say the least, a situation in which he might be driven down on to the *Falls of Dochart* and thus bring about her end. But it might be possible by use of his engines—just so long as the bearings didn't overheat again.

When he was as close as he dared go, he ordered the engines stopped. Now through his binoculars he was able to make out men on the fo'c'sle. Chatto, probably, and another, perhaps the passenger who had been reported as so foolishly going over the side to join Chatto's boarding party.

He lifted his megaphone, shouted across the water. There was no response.

As predicted by Patience, the *Falls of Dochart* had now broached-to. She lay in the trough, was lifted to the summit, again and again, lying broadside to the sea, the great waves dropping with immense force from stem to stern, from poop to fo'c'sle.

If those waves should penetrate the cargo hatches the end would come fast. Once the fore hatch had been cleared of its rice cargo, Tom had found spare canvas below in the sail locker, and a makeshift tarpaulin had been rigged over the hatch and well chocked down with wedges driven in by a carpenter's mallet. That might hold, or it might not.

'It won't if this goes on for long,' Patience shouted into Tom's ear. 'There's no canvas ever made, that can go on taking that sort of strain, not without the backing of wooden hatchcovers.'

Tom nodded, keeping his feet with immense difficulty on the plunging deck, gripping the lifeline to stop himself being hurled overboard. 'Any suggestions?' he shouted across the wind. Suggestions were not very likely: the situation, and this he had to face, was impossible. They could never come through now.

But Patience did have a suggestion. 'Make sail,' he shouted.

Tom stared at him. 'How, for God's sake? What with?'

'Spare suit of sails in the sail locker, boy, the fair-weather ones. The weather may not be fair...but they'll have to do. What do you say?' Patience bared his teeth in a devilish grin. 'You're the boss—you said!'

Tom looked aloft. 'What about the masts?'

'We still have most of the mainmast, boy. And the yards. We can jury-rig a maincourse and maybe a lower tops'l as well. Might be enough to get us head to wind and keep us there until the blow moderates—'

'Fine—if we could steer.' Tom waved a hand aft to where the wheel had been smashed away before his party had boarded.

'We jury-rig the bloody rudder, boy, that's what! Pulley-hauley on the rudder-head. Do you go along with that—or don't you?'

Tom was about to answer when Patience gave a shout, and pointed over the port side. Swinging round, Tom saw the loom of the liner, a vast lit-up shape appearing out of the foam and the spindrift, looking as though it was about to crash down on top of them.

Watching through a murky dawn as with tricky engine shifts ahead and astern he held the liner off in as much safety as possible, Fullbright saw figures moving along the decks of the windjammer and going below, apparently to the storage spaces beneath the raised fo'c'sle. He watched in alarm and wonderment: this was no time for anyone to go below, to be perhaps caught in a confined space when the vessel finally went down. Shortly after this, four men emerged on to the fore deck, staggering under a heavy weight. Carrying something, something long and heavy... Fullbright ticked over, and turned to Forster who had left the now useless tow and had come to the bridge.

'They're bringing up sail,' he said in astonishment. 'They're going to try to get sail on her!'

Forster grunted. 'A waste of time if you ask me, sir.'

'I didn't ask you, Mr Forster, but I'll give you an answer: it may not be a waste of time, in my opinion. Chatto's a good hand and—wasn't there something about that passenger?'

'Sivyer, yes. Believed to be a seaman, done time in sail. Just a rumour.'

'That augurs well if it's true. We'll wish them luck, Mr Forster. In the meantime I'll hold the ship between them and the weather, give them such lee as is possible.' Fullbright knew he couldn't put his ship square across the weather; that would mean bringing her across the greybeards and risking being broached-to himself. The best he could do was to keep his ship ahead of the windjammer, keep her head to the wind, and rely on his beam to deflect at least some of the weight of wind.

This he did; and ordered the Chief Officer back to stand by aft. Just in case. Another tow might be needed yet if the windjammer survived the night, and the next day, and the day after that...

Full daylight brought the expected deluge once again to the purser's office and once again a surge of passengers to the vantage points from which they could rubberneck men's efforts to save a ship and their own lives.

Some of them became belligerent when told by the stewards, and then by the officers, to obey the already given order to remain off the open decks. When reports to this effect reached the bridge, Fullbright handed over to the First Officer and went below himself to exert the authority of his gold-leafed cap and the four gold stripes on the shoulders of his bridge coat. Passengers must obey orders as must the crew. Everything was for their own safety.

They respected the Captain's authority: they mostly knew that his position as Master of the ship meant just that, and he had the power to confine disobedience to its cabin, or in extreme cases to cells.

He was met, when making his way through the first-class lounge back to the bridge, by the most recalcitrant, the most infuriatingly tiresome of them all, attended by her long-suffering maid.

'Oh, Captain. Just the very person I wished to see, how very fortunate.'

Fullbright was pretty certain she had been lying in wait for him. 'Good morning, Lady Moyra. How can I help you?'

'Another delay,' she said. Her jaw, Fullbright noted not for the first time, was like a rat-trap. 'It's one thing after another and really it's not good enough. We simply haven't *moved* for goodness knows how long and—'

'Necessity, Lady Moyra. A disabled ship—'

'Oh, yes, yes, I know all that, how could I not?' She waved a hand impatiently at the

Falls of Dochart, preparing now a makeshift maincourse and main lower tops'l, though the niceties of this escaped her. 'I'd not have thought it worth...oh, well,' she added, seeing the set of Fullbright's face, 'perhaps I'd better not say any more about that to a sailor. But it's not right that passengers should be so put out, surely you must see that? No one seems able to tell me when we shall arrive in Valparaiso. Perhaps you'd be good enough to do so, Captain Fullbright?'

Fullbright held on to his temper—just. 'I'm afraid I can't, Lady Moyra—'

'You, the Captain, do not know?'

'No, I don't. It depends on many things. My own engines, what happens to the windjammer astern, the weather... I am unable to make any estimate at all at this moment, Lady Moyra.'

'But the Captain must surely—'

'The Captain must not surely anything, Lady Moyra. I suggest you consult a higher authority than myself.' Fullbright made to move away but was restrained by a skinny hand clutching at his arm.

'Who would that be?' Lady Moyra asked.

'God,' Fullbright snapped. 'Prayer would

258

not come amiss in any case. I suggest you try it.'

The hand dropped. Fullbright strode on through the lounge. Lady Moyra was gasping like a fish. 'What a *rude* man,' she managed to say to Connolly. 'I shall report him the *moment* we reach Valparaiso...'

Aboard the windjammer, work had begun on attaching heavy ropes to either side of the rudder-head, which lay some feet below the water.

Patience had volunteered for the job of going over the stern, tended by a lifeline from the deck. Tom had refused; he was the younger man and he would do the job himself. On that, he was insistent. Patience would be better employed taking charge on deck.

Such precautions as were possible were taken. The lifeline was attached to Tom's body, the noose held beneath his arms on a bowline and the inboard end led around a belaying pin on the poop with two hands to back it up. Heavier ropes were made ready, to be lowered over into the turbulent water when Tom was in position to make the attachment to the port and starboard arms of the rudder-head.

When there was enough light, Tom stood by the after rail, one leg over above the surge of water.

'All ready, Mr Patience?'

'All ready, boy, all ready. And good luck go with you—for all our sakes.'

Tom got a grip on the lifeline, jerked at it to ensure that its inboard end was fast, and dropped down into the water.

FIFTEEN

The passengers aboard the *Orvega* were being kept informed as to what was going on aboard the windjammer. Fullbright had let it be known that his Second Officer was in charge and was working manfully to get the disabled vessel to rights. Fullbright made no reference to heroism: in his book, a seaman did his job to the best of his ability and that was that. But all the passengers could read into the situation that if Chatto succeeded, then a hero was what he would be.

Grace Handley was in no doubt on the point. She already had much time for Tom Chatto, regretting only that he had not been more forthcoming during the voyage. When—if—he returned aboard he would be lionized... That lady friend of his, Dolores something...she was a lucky girl. If he stuck to her. Maybe he wouldn't; they were still a long way from Valparaiso. Young Mr Chatto might yet be made more malleable. Grace Handley was well aware that he was attracted to her.

Tidy and Bolsover discussed the overall situation. 'I'm glad it's not me in that boat,' Tidy said. 'I take my hat off to that young man. He'll go far in the Line's service, shouldn't wonder.' He paused, scratching his chin. 'Odd, about that bloke Sivyer. Wouldn't have thought it of him. Curious bloke...didn't strike me as, well, any sort of a hero.'

'You never know, do you? Some rise to a situation, others don't. He did, for some reason.' Bolsover looked across the heaving lounge, saw Grace Handley coming in by the for'ard door from the main lobby outside the purser's office. He lowered his voice. 'Hazard number one—for our Mr Chatto.'

'Eh? What is?'

'Don't look now...Mrs Handley. Got her

261

sights on him, as we all know. Or have guessed, anyway. Snake in the grass, I'd say. Chatto's intended—Dolores—I doubt if she's the sort to turn a blind eye, not even to a shipboard romance. And Pontarena certainly wouldn't.'

'Are they ever likely to know?'

Bolsover said, 'Old man Pontarena has eyes and ears everywhere. I've said before—he's powerful.' He saw Tidy's sudden sardonic expression. 'Don't look at me, I'd never say a word. What people do is their own affair, and anyway I'm broad-minded, even if Pontarena isn't. For now—'nough said.' Grace Handley had seen them, and was coming across. She stopped, as if by chance. It was, as Bolsover knew, quite likely that young Chatto had told the woman that he, Bolsover, was acquainted with the Pontarena family. Mrs Handley might be on a probing expedition; Bolsover clammed right up.

The icy cold was in Tom's very bones; only the urgency and sheer hard physical work had kept his blood circulating. The men of the windjammers were accustomed to working in freezing conditions, working canvas and cordage with frozen fingers, and often enough up to their waists in water when working on deck. He plunged beneath the surface, and came up again, time after time, trying desperately to fumble the heavy rope over the arm of the rudder-head and make it fast. The job seemed to take an age. Each time he fancied he had got the rope over, there was a surge of water and it slid free again. His teeth chattered; his hands were numb, useless, but he struggled on. The job had to be done and that was all about it. He recalled something he had once heard in connection with he couldn't remember what: *The difficult we do at once, the impossible takes a little longer.*

A hell of a lot longer; he was almost at his last gasp. Then he saw legs coming over the after rail above. Patience, disobeying orders. Patience, with ability and determination written all over his face.

He hung on the surface as Patience came down alongside him.

'All right, boy, you've done fine. But now let daddy lend a bloody hand.'

It was done at last. Tom wasn't currently reckoning time. The ropes secured, they climbed back on to the poop. The ropes were led through the fairleads on either side and the few available hands were detailed to take up the slack and then belay each rope around the cleats. After that, largely under Patience's direction, the canvas that had been brought from the sail locker and made ready was sent aloft. It was a gut-tearing, fingernail-wrenching business to set the maincourse and main lower tops'l, a manoeuvre conducted in the teeth of the gale, though the force of the wind was from time to time deflected by the wavetops themselves. The relevant sheets and guys and downhauls were rove through the blocks ready to haul the canvas round as necessary to meet the wind if and when the ship could be brought by her makeshift steering back from her broached-to position, brought across the greybeards to head into them and take the sea fore-and-aft along her deck rather than have the weight of water drop flat on the struggling seamen.

When all was ready Tom passed the orders to haul the helm over and, under the power of the jury-rigged sails, make the attempt to bring the ship across the waves to resume her comparatively safe heading. Muscle and sweat; and the sheer determination brought about by the overriding urgency of getting the ship round before she became a totally waterlogged derelict. All that, plus guts.

Unbelievably, they did it in the end. Time and again they were thrown back; time and again they made the next attempt. Their eventual success was seen from the liner. The first to see it was the Captain, watching from monkey's island. He gave a shout, snatched off his cap and waved it. He couldn't be heard, but he called out just the same.

'Well done, Chatto. Brilliant work! On the part of you all. I'm proud of the lot of you.'

The word spread among the passengers that something not far short of a miracle had been performed aboard the windjammer. Groups talked excitedly in all three classes. In the steerage they talked about Sivyer. Difficult bastard, was the general verdict, and not wholly trustworthy. But he'd turned up trumps just the same.

'Thank goodness,' Lady Moyra said snappishly. 'Now perhaps we shall move on.'

With the ship heading into wind and sea, with the canvas giving them way to tack across the westerlies, they rode more or less easily. Not yet out of the wood, though. Patience didn't need to give his warning: 'We've yet to find a shift of wind to carry us on, boy. We can't tack for ever...we'll be blown back easterly.' He paused. 'Maybe if the wind drops, we'll pick up the tow again.'

'Yes. But there's something else first: Captain Lee. The body...it'll have to go over the side.'

There were, of course, considerations of the law's requirements. No doctor had attended, no death certificate had been issued. Patience said that didn't matter. There were always deaths aboard a sailing ship. 'And never a doctor. The shore authorities, they'll take our word, never fear. They always do.'

Tom caught Patience's eye, saw the sudden flicker. Patience felt he'd been too forthcoming, perhaps recalling his own part years before in the death of a seaman. But no time for either of them to dwell on that: the body of the windjammer's late Master must go overboard with as much dignity as possible, though in the current circumstances there would be little of that available. Not even a canvas shroud: there was no sailmaker aboard, and Patience's skills didn't run to the use of a sailmaker's palm and needle. Captain Lee's body was already dressed in monkey jacket and coarse trousers: the cold of the cabin, with fires drawn long since, had been too intense to allow anything but turning in all standing. The body was brought up to the poop by Patience and the apprentice and laid upon a broken plank from the wreckage of the tween-deck.

Tom said the only prayer he knew: the Lord's Prayer. That was all: he had no idea as to what passage from the old man's Bible he could have appropriately read. At Tom's nod the plank was tilted and the body dropped formlessly into the storm-tossed water, to be carried away easterly by the greybeards of the Horn, to float half submerged for a while and then finally sink.

A lonely end but perhaps a fitting one, and one that the old windjammer captain might have chosen for himself.

Under the inadequate jury-rig they made little if any westerly progress, being forced to tack, ceaselessly as it seemed, seeking for that vital shift of wind to carry them on. With no navigation aids to help them—the steering compass and the binnacle had been carried away with the wheel—no proper assessment could be made of their position. Cape Horn and the coastline to the north had vanished, an indication that there was a southerly drift; but how strong that drift was could not be calculated.

Southward lay the ice. The worries that had been Fullbright's now became Tom's. He spoke of this to Patience.

'Don't worry before you have to, boy. The liner's still in contact.' The *Orvega* was standing by, keeping some four cable's-lengths ahead of the windjammer. 'She'll send a message by the semaphore if we look like standing into danger of too much drift.'

That was true. Tom gave himself a mental shake. He should have known; he was desperately tired. And although the weather, having worsened since the tow had been passed, was currently making it impossible for Fullbright to send away a boat, another tow would surely be passed as soon as conditions permitted.

During the night Patience, taking the watch while Tom caught up on some sleep, was heard shouting down the hatch that led from the poop to the cabin and the saloon. Tom woke on the instant and went up the ladder at the rush.

Patience was pointing towards the main lower tops'l, just visible, white against the dark. 'We've got the shift, Mister Chatto! Get you to the sheets, and loose her just a little. Now's our chance.'

They ran to where the lower tops'l sheets were secured to a belaying pin on the storm-battered bulwarks. The sail was hauled round, together now with the maincourse. At once the ship rode more easily, taking up the wind's shift, and began to make westerly progress across the scend of the sea. By morning they were moving steadily ahead; and once the visibility was enough for a semaphore message to be read aboard the liner, Tom went for'ard to the bows. His wave was acknowledged from the *Orvega's* bridge; he passed his message, reporting the shift of wind. Soon after, a message came back to him. There had been some drift; he was advised to stand a few miles northward.

'Follow my movements,' Fullbright's message ended.

As the liner altered course west-nor'-west, Tom, back on the poop with the hands manning the ropes secured to the rudderhead, and Patience and the apprentice ready at the sheets, brought the windjammer's head up to keep in station astern of the liner. His spirits rose; he believed now that they were going to make it.

'Don't count chickens,' Patience said dourly later. 'You've had enough experience of these parts to know you're not in the clear until you're out into the Pacific.'

Those words turned out to be prophetic.

The time was coming for Fullbright to move towards some ahead decisions. He conferred with Harrison, Forster and Ainsworth. Harrison was still concerned about his engines, back to working on a single screw at a time.

'Will they get us to Valparaiso, Chief?'

Harrison shrugged. 'I can't say for sure, sir. They may, but I can't guarantee it. They're not doing themselves any good.' He looked speculatively at Fullbright. 'Are you thinking you may take her into Puerto Montt?'

Fullbright pursed his lips. The Chilean port of Puerto Montt lay around eight hundred miles north of the Magellan Strait. 'Perhaps, Chief. I wouldn't like to risk an engine-room breakdown off the Chilean coast. There are rocks aplenty, and to stand farther off the coast into the Pacific would increase the distance to Valparaiso. If we entered Puerto Montt, it would take six hundred miles *off.*'

'That would help,' Harrison said. 'If you're asking me, sir, I'd say Puerto Montt.'

'Even if they haven't the capacity to effect a full repair?'

'Yes, I'd say so. Parts can be sent down from Valparaiso if necessary. Of course, it'll mean a very considerable delay on the Valparaiso arrival.'

'Yes, indeed.' Fullbright turned to Ainsworth. 'I'm making no final decision yet—a lot depends on the *Falls of Dochart,* of course. But you'd better have it in mind that we may need to feed the ship for longer than you may have stocked up for. I'll assume we can embark provisions in Puerto Montt...and I'll leave you to cope with the complaints, all right?'

Ainsworth grinned. 'There'll be plenty of them, sir, that's for sure. Some of them may want to leave the ship and travel overland to Valparaiso—if so, that can be arranged—'

'Sooner them than me,' Fullbright said with a laugh. 'It's a case of coach-and-horses, I believe, and bandits along the way, but that'll be their choice, not mine.' Fullbright paused. 'What's the mood among the passengers now, Ainsworth?'

'Mostly understanding, sir. They recognize the necessity, and they're concerned about the windjammer. And about Chatto. He's made himself popular among the passengers. The one outstanding fly in the ointment is Lady Moyra Bentinck. I think most of the first-class would like to jettison her overboard.'

'So would I,' Fullbright said with feeling.

There had been much talk about Tom Chatto among the passengers, admiration for what he was doing aboard the windjammer being the subject of discussion. Lady Moyra had become increasingly irritated with mention of Tom's name. After all, he was doing no more than his job as ordered by

Captain Fullbright; she really didn't know what all the fuss was about. Also, what was being done for the wretched sailing ship, no more than a derelict that should have been left alone to sink, was preventing her own arrival at Valparaiso. That, in her mind, could be laid at the door of that young man.

She grew vengeful; the more vengeful the more she concentrated on her woes, the more she heard about Mr Chatto—Chatto this and Chatto that. Such nonsense it all was.

And there was that Mrs Handley, who was no better than she should be. There had been talk; and she had seen them together. She didn't like Mrs Handley, who was common and inclined to be impertinent.

That young man had had no business to be consorting with any passenger. Lady Moyra's jaw set. Mrs Handley was the young man's Achilles' heel. Not that Lady Moyra saw any way in which she could make positive use of that fact. Not yet, anyway. But it was a thought. She was sure Captain Fullbright must know what was going on, or had been going on, and would no doubt go on again when the young man rejoined the liner. Captain Fullbright—such a rude man—could be said to run an immoral ship...and it was nothing short of scandalous for him to have invoked God when she had asked him a simple question.

'Connolly.'

'Yes, me lady?'

'Get off your bottom and go and fetch me some writing paper. And a pen and ink. No, a pencil will be better, the ship is so unsteady.'

Things were better committed to paper while they were fresh in the mind. Connolly returned with the writing materials.

'Put them on my dressing table. No. Bring that small table over here. That's better. Don't go away, Connolly.'

'Sorry, me lady. I was just—'

'Oh, never mind what you were just, girl! Go and find Mrs Handley. No, better still, since you won't have the gumption to find out which of the passengers she is...go to the purser's office and say I wish a message delivered, a verbal one. I would appreciate it if Mrs Handley could be told I would like her to come to my stateroom for tea. This afternoon, Connolly. Now, do you understand all that, or do you not?'

'Yes, me lady.'

'Very well, then off you go. And do try not to look so dreadfully *dreary*, girl, it's so depresssing.'

The message, reaching Grace Handley, caused astonishment. What did the old besom want with her? One answer was obvious enough: nothing good. Grace knew what Lady Moyra's opinion of her was—it was unmistakable in the way she looked at her, down her aristocratic nose. But, intrigued, she would obey the summons.

SIXTEEN

'There are things,' Patience said carefully, 'that I can't forget.'

Tom and Patience had gone below to the dead captain's cabin abaft the saloon, leaving the ship's apprentice in charge of the hands on deck. Lee's belongings had to be gone through and, if possible, some address found of a next of kin, if there was one. Tom would write a letter, telling whoever it might be—a wife, a son, a daughter, a sister or brother perhaps—of the old man's end and the fact that in life he had never left his ship in danger. Now Tom looked up at Patience. The former First Mate was glancing around the cabin, perhaps thinking of what might have been, and there was a regretful sound in his voice.

Tom said, 'No point in going back into the past, Mr Patience.'

Patience had got his drift. 'Not that far back, boy. Things more recent. I'm not proud of myself... I had it in for you. But you know that.'

Tom said nothing; just waited. Patience went on: 'Threats. Oh, I meant them—then! Not any more. You've done a man's job aboard this floating coffin. But it's not just that, you see. I don't want to peg out with what's on my conscience.'

'Forget it,' Tom said. He was uneasy; this conversation was not like Patience, Patience the bully, the hard-case mate, the killer of the French stowaway years before. It seemed that he was bringing himself to the sort of deathbed confession he'd begun some days earlier, as though he was really expectant of death. That feeling grew as Patience went into a rambling description, another confession, that it had been he who had attacked the cabman back in Buenos Aires outside the home of Dolores Pontarena's aunt; this merged into an account of an injured woman, a steerage passenger in the *Orvega,* whom Patience had robbed of money as she lay on the deck.

'She died soon after, boy. Like robbing a corpse...to think I could do a thing like that. I've seen myself, boy, I've seen myself...like in a mirror. Seen myself plain. Being back aboard a windjammer, I don't know...' His voice trailed away and, to Tom's embarrassment, he put his head in his hands and his body shook with sobs.

There was nothing Tom could do, nothing he could say. After a while Patience quietened. He looked up at Tom. 'Off my chest,' he said. 'It's a relief. I pray God'll forgive me, that's all.'

Lady Moyra oozed charm, a synthetic charm with a purpose behind it as Grace Handley could see well enough. The afternoon tea, provided by Lady Moyra's cabin stewardess and administered by Connolly, was lavish. China tea or Indian, freshly baked scones with strawberry jam, sandwiches, thinly cut bread and butter, luscious cakes of many varieties.

'*So* good of you to come, my dear Mrs Handley.'

Grace smiled with a hint of ice. 'Royal command, no option.'

A haughty stiffening of backbone. 'I beg your pardon? No, please don't repeat what you said. I believe it was rudely meant.'

Grace said casually, 'Someone once said that a gentleman—or lady—was one who was rude only when he or she meant to be.'

'And you're no lady, Mrs Handley.'

Gloves off. 'Perhaps not, Lady Moyra. Also, I'm no adulteress.'

Lady Moyra's face darkened in a flush. 'I wonder, Mrs Handley. *I wonder!* You and that young Second Officer—Mr Chatto as I understand. Something has been going on and that you simply cannot deny—'

'Yes, I can. And I do. A shipboard friendship, nothing more. And you're a wicked old woman.'

'I—'

Grace Handley got to her feet, face flaming, her temper out of control. 'If you make any mischief for Tom, I'll see to it that your name's dragged through the mud in Valparaiso and anywhere else in Chile you may be going to. It's a Catholic country and they don't like titled bitches who go for a bang with their husbands' brother officers—so there!'

Lady Moyra was almost speechless; but not quite. 'There is such a thing as the law of slander,' she said.

'Yes, I do know that, and it works both ways. But, you see, since you are accusing me of something that has never happened, you have no proof to offer. I, on the other hand, along with the whole ship, know for sure what you got up to in South Africa.'

Lady Moyra raised her stick, her face contorted. But Mrs Handley stormed out of the stateroom in time.

Lady Moyra had a mottled look. A deflated balloon, she tried to struggle up from her chair but fell back, gasping. Connolly, who had heard the whole exchange through the bulkhead dividing the sitting room from the pantry, heard it with glee. A real put-down; her dreadful lady would never survive that. With any luck she would have a fit.

By now the weather was moderating. The

ships rode easier and made more speed. However, Fullbright suspected another blow lurking ahead, towards the west, a blow that, if it materialized, would meet them inwards of the turn north into the Pacific.

Fullbright's weather sense was confirmed when signals were exchanged with a steamship on the easterly passage, making for Cape Horn from Valparaiso: there was a strong nor'-westerly blow developing.

'Trouble for the windjammer,' Fullbright said. 'She's doing well enough under her jury-rig, but she won't be well placed if there's more dirty weather. Now's the moment to pass another tow, Mr Forster.'

A message was sent to the *Falls of Dochart.* On receipt, Tom began to make preparations for taking the tow. Patience, who seemed to have recovered his spirits somewhat, worked with him. At the liner's counter men could soon be seen standing ready by the ropes, while the griping bands were cast off the seaboat which was then lowered on the falls to pull round to the stern.

With flatter seas, the manoeuvre was completed in less time than before. Tom decided to leave the jury-rigged sails in place; they might help to reduce the strain on the towing pendant.

From now on it should be easy. Tom said as much. Patience didn't answer. He didn't look well; there had been an emaciated look about him when Tom had first seen him embarking aboard the liner in Liverpool. Now it was much more marked. Food, of course, had been scarce aboard the windjammer—nothing but hard tack and ship's biscuits—only just up to subsistence level, but Patience's drawn look went deeper than that, Tom thought. A question more of age and lack of muscle-hardening exercise in the lean years ashore. Or of Patience's mind. Although seeming easier, he was still obviously under some sort of mental strain. As for food, they would eat better for a while at least: the *Orvega's* seaboat had brought provisions: tinned milk, ditto soup that would have to be drunk cold, and tinned ham. Also, a bottle of brandy.

They had both eyed the brandy.

'Medicinal use only, Mr Patience.'

'Sure thing, boy! Sure thing!'

Tom wasn't quite so sure about Patience. But he just had to hope for reasonableness.

It would be rather too pointed if he were to lock the bottle away in the saloon.

However, there would be no harm in a snifter for all hands. They had all earned it. Tom passed the bottle from mouth to mouth, keeping a hold of it. It wasn't much, but it brought a glow of warmth to cheer men who had had no comfort for days past. The small drink taken, Patience went off to sound round the ship below, a task he had undertaken a number of times already, one that had constantly to be done. Leaks had been plugged as effectively as possible, but each time Patience went below there were more to be dealt with. The old ship had been badly hit by the storm and in Patience's view she was scarcely worth the saving, worth men's lives. But he was a seaman yet, and would do his best while he lived. Fullbright had signalled his probable intention to take the liner into Puerto Montt for engine repairs and if he did so would send a boat inshore to request entry and the services of two tugs, one for the *Orvega* herself and one to take over the windjammer, which would be cast off on the tug's arrival.

Patience had entered Puerto Montt years before in sail, also under guidance of a tug. 'It's a tricky entry,' he'd said to Tom. 'Rocks and shallows. I'd not like to attempt it in a big steamship, but I suppose Fullbright knows what he's doing. He'll have seen the charts and he'll know the depth of water—and his own draught.'

Now, coming up from his inspection, he pondered. Port had seemed a long way off; but it loomed closer now that entry was being discussed in detail. He wondered what awaited him: he had made that confession to Chatto, made it out of the gloom and despair of his mind. Chatto might make use of it or he might not. Patience believed he would not; it had been told as a confidence, and young Chatto was the sort of man to respect that. But his conscience remained, and the fear. Some information, as he had suspected much earlier aboard the *Orvega,* might have come through from Buenos Aires to Valparaiso, and when the authorities got the word that the liner was entering Puerto Montt, that information might be sent south by the telegraph.

The reports from the engine room were not good; Fullbright made the final decision to enter Puerto Montt. To do so was, as Patience had known, tricky; but not impossible. Since the 1850s there had been a strong German presence in the port, which was the capital of the province of Llanquihue; and according to the Admiralty's Sailing Directions, squadrons of German warships had entered Reloncavi Bay from time to time. If the Germans could do it, then so could he.

Together with Forster, who in Chatto's absence would act as navigator, he examined the charts, plotting his inward course. There would be an undeniable risk of grounding, and to go aground with a full passenger list would not be funny. Warnings would have to be given to the passengers: there must be no substantial gathering of gawpers to one side or the other, for instance, such that might give the ship even the smallest list at a dangerous moment. His officers would be instructed to ensure that.

He straightened from the chart table and made his way back to the bridge. As he did so, he noted the long, low line of cloud ahead, very black cloud in a sky that had begun to clear of the Cape Horn weather.

'The blow's coming, Mr Forster. Not

long, either. Keep an eye lifting on the tow, if you please. And the usual precautions aboard.'

Forster acknowledged. The anchor cables on the fo'c'sle would be checked, the slips tightened where necessary and extra strops put in place. The lifeboats' falls and griping bands would be similarly checked and as the storm approached all ports would be clamped down hard behind their deadlights. Forster, going aft to make sure that all was well with the tow, looked again at the horizon ahead: he didn't like the look of that low, very black cloud, now with menacing streaks of colour coming from it. There was a kind of foreboding in that sight; and overall there was a sort of hush, an absence of sound that seemed to hang in the air like a harbinger of doom.

Ahead, as Forster knew well, were the Diego Ramirez rocks, the graveyard of very many sailing vessels and their crews.

Tom had seen the horizon. Patience had agreed with his assessment of it.

'Dangerous, boy. Unusual, too, from that quarter. I don't like it. Sudden squalls...'

There was no need to elaborate. Tom

knew what sudden squalls could do to a windjammer, but there was comfort in being under tow. But comfort of a sort only: Tom already had good reason to know that tows could part under the strain of being jerked from the water when the two ships plunged and dipped to the sea.

The line of black extended rapidly. It seemed like an express train as it roared down from ahead. When it hit the ships it was accompanied by teeming rain that came down with such force that it literally bounced back up from the deck. The maincourse and lower tops'l shook, tearing at the cringles. Tom cupped his hands against the batter of the wind and shouted at Patience.

'Better get the canvas off her...it's doing no good now!'

Patience agreed. All hands went to the sheets and downhauls. The sails were loosed from their reefs by the few hands, their stomachs pressed to the yards, their feet sliding on the foot ropes as they grappled the wet, heavy canvas. Working with desperation now, the young apprentice was struck full in the face by the flap of the lower tops'l as it ripped and flailed madly to starboard. He lost his grip of the yard, and slid from the foot rope, arms flung out, face contorted. Tom heard the scream as the youngster took the guardrail on the flat of his back, then went over the side to be lost almost at once in the raging foam that now surrounded the ship.

Tom ran to the side. Patience shouted at him, 'Nothing to be done, boy! He's beyond all help, and has likely broken his back.'

With work to be done, Tom had to thrust it from his mind. A moment later the lower tops'l went the same way, ripping from the cringles to vanish, flapping wildly, away to starboard, sails and chains and wires flying around in all directions with a noise like artillery. It was a case, simply, of far too few hands; but the maincourse was taken off safely after a hard struggle.

Tom could only pray that the tow would hold. Like Forster, he was remembering the sharp teeth of Diego Ramirez.

Fullbright watched with growing concern. The storm was playing havoc with his own ship; the open decks were swept with the wind's fury and the vicious rain, with the mounting seas that came over the bow, washed aft along the fo'c'sle to drop thunderously down on to the fore well-deck with a force likely, if it kept up too long, to smash the hatch-cover and flood the fore holds, thence perhaps to spread out along the adjacent decks with the prospect of a loss of buoyancy unless the pumps could cope. Two of the lifeboats on the port side had been stoved in by the crashing weight of water swirling up the ship's side to drop down on the boat deck. Pleas had come from the starting platform; as a result Fullbright had reduced speed again, keeping the revolutions just high enough to maintain his course, heading dead into wind and sea.

Below, battened down behind the dead-lights of the cabins, with essential water-tight doors closed on the order from the bridge, the passengers suffered. The steerage decks were a shambles, a heaving hell as the ship rose and fell alarmingly, rolling heavily at the same time to produce a vicious corkscrew motion. Vomit was everywhere, even urine where some of the men and women had been too ill to move to the lavatories. Furnishings lay smashed, cabins had become prisons to be kept out of when possible, the dining saloon remained empty. There was no food even for those who might want it—no hot food, for the galley fires had been drawn earlier. The passengers existed in a foul, cold fug. The only warmth now was in the engine and boiler rooms. In the latter the trimmers and firemen cursed furiously as they were thrown against the furnaces, or found burning coal from the furnace-mouths pursuing them across the steel deck-plates.

There were more injuries for Dr Murphy to attend to: one of them was Lieutenant and Quartermaster Tidy, who had slipped in an alleyway while conveying a bottle of whisky from Bolsover's cabin to his own, in the interest of a nightcap. The bottle had not been full, but its loss was a blow; and its glass, in breaking under Tidy's weight, had done damage to his leg. He bled profusely and was patched up by the nursing sister, who reported the presence of drink to the doctor.

'I don't blame him,' Murphy said. 'I'd be boozed myself if I wasn't the doctor...' But he made a mental note that, if it should come to abandoning, not in fact likely in such a sea, Tidy would probably need to be poured into the lifeboat.

No passengers bothered the purser's

staff: they were not risking unnecessary movement around the decks, even though lifelines had been rigged in all appropriate places throughout the accommodation. The lounges, writing rooms and bars were dreary places now, the wind-lashed rain and the spray beating up against the square ports giving on to the deserted promenade deck. Wind howled round the funnel stays and the standing rigging, making a weird and premonitory sighing sound. Even the seagulls that had accompanied the ship for most of her voyage, waiting for the galleys to discharge their waste, were absent. The ship was isolated in the wastes of the southern sea. Lady Moyra lay in her bunk like death itself, her stomach emptied by continual seasickness, calling time and again for Connolly who was in little better state herself but was forced to keep going. She had noted that her mistress had gone into what she called a decline ever since the abortive tea-party with Mrs Handley. Connolly wished her ill, vengefully, but knew she would recover: the wicked always got away with it.

Frequent reports reached Fullbright, keeping constantly to the bridge, as to the state of things below. The crew's quarters beneath the fo'c'sle had suffered: water coming into the well-deck had flooded into the mess room and the sleeping berths with their tiered bunks. Similarly aft: water had entered the steerage to add to the misery. These apart, the ship was sound. The carpenter reported no leakage, and the double bottoms contained no more than their normal, messy, smelly sludge.

Fullbright's chief concern was the windjammer and the men aboard her. So far, the tow was holding, though there was immense strain on the towing pendant, which lifted continually from the water. When night came down, it was no longer possible, in the prevailing poor visibility, to see the towing pendant; or to see the windjammer herself other than as an occasional white blur of foam as she lifted to the crests.

In the midnight to 4.00 a.m. watch the First Officer reported, 'We should be almost due south of the Diego Ramirez, sir.'

Fullbright brought up his binoculars and focused them to starboard. The First Officer said, 'You'll not see them, sir. I calculated by dead reckoning.'

'I hope to God we *don't* see them,'

Fullbright said. 'Once we're past...well, it'll be one less worry.'

The Diego Ramirez were invisible also from the *Falls of Dochart,* where Tom and Patience were both remaining on deck; they would stay there throughout the old ship's ordeal. Their few fo'c'sle hands were taking it in watches to stand by the tow, two of them at a time being handy in case of need, of some sudden emergency.

It was at two bells in the four to eight watch, the time of the lowest human ebb and a time of darkness so thick that it seemed almost tangible, that the trouble struck. It struck with devastating suddenness, as disasters tended to do. No warning: just a violent movement of the fo'c'sle, a waggle of the ship's hull, and a terrifying noise from the starboard bow. Something vast flew past Tom's head, missing him by a fraction. There was a heavy clanging noise, apparently from the bullring in the eyes of the ship, following a splintering noise from right alongside the spot where Patience had been standing; then more splintering from right ahead as the ship fell off the wind and sea and lay wallowing in the trough.

Tom, utterly bewildered, realized only one thing at first: the tow had parted again. Within the next minute he saw the full extent: the tow had not so much parted as pulled clear out of the ship. Rotting woodwork on the fo'c'sle had allowed the weight of the tow to wrench the starboard bitts right out; the bitts had struck the bullring, the towing pendant had slipped free, and the bitts, very heavy twin iron bollards, had catapulted over the bow to smash away the bowsprit before dropping down into the sea.

There was no sight of Patience. Tom turned aft, shouted down wind. There was no reply. Then, moving to the side, his seabooted feet slid on something sticky. He fell, rolled towards the guardrail, almost went overboard but saved himself with an outflung arm just in time. Upright again, holding fast to the lifeline, he half stumbled once more and, recovering himself, saw Patience, his head shattered, no doubt by the full impact of the bitts hurtling to the strain of the towing pendant, his body held by a projection in the deck, beneath the starboard anchor secured to the cathead, until it was

taken overboard by the surge of the
sea.

Then, with the wind's shriek cut off
by the wave-crests rearing overhead, Tom
became aware of another sound: the crash
and boom of waves breaking on rock. Not
far distant, off the starboard quarter.

Diego Ramirez for a certainty.

SEVENTEEN

'Tow parted, sir!'

Fullbright slammed back the voicepipe
cover and rang down for an emergency
stop on the engines, his face grim. He
had the same alternatives as before: he
could turn the ship, steam back to see
what he could do, which wouldn't be
much, if anything at all, in the sea that
was running. And to do that would be to
risk broaching—to as he came across the
wind and sea. The Diego Ramirez were
not far off astern. The potential danger
to his passengers and crew must, above
all, be borne in mind. Upwards of twelve
hundred souls in his charge, as against

a handful aboard the windjammer. The life-saving instincts of the sea held good; but any Captain had to consider the larger good. And that lay in numbers.

The other alternative was to hold his course.

It was unlikely that anybody aboard the windjammer would survive for long. The decision was in fact quite plain; it had to be. Plain, but utterly abhorrent. The lot of many a master mariner over the long years of Britain's maritime story.

Forster came to the bridge to report in person. The rudder and screws were clear and the towing pendant itself had been found to be intact. Something had come adrift aboard the windjammer. Forster asked, 'What will you do, sir?' Something in his voice told Fullbright that he already knew the inevitable answer.

'I shall hold my course,' Fullbright said heavily.

The word had spread by morning. The decks buzzed with comment. The Captain had behaved inhumanly, disregarding life, disregarding shipwrecked seamen, in dishonour of his calling. He would not be able to live with himself thereafter; in the meantime he should be shunned by the passengers, ostracized, a pariah.

The ship's officers and crew told a different story. They were men of the sea and understood the Captain's agony of mind, and they stood by him. It was likely they all owed their lives to him. The Captain was to be commiserated with, except that none of the crew would be so insensitive as to do so.

Not all the passengers followed the sheep's lead. They saw the correctness of a hard decision. One was Bolsover, a man who had travelled the seas from Liverpool to South America many times. Another was Grace Handley, shedding a tear in private for Tom Chatto. He'd had a good future before him; but he'd left it behind him in honour, in doing his job to the very end. She would miss him; but she felt a sense of pride. And, like Tom, Captain Fullbright had done the right and only thing. Believing that, knowing that, she did her best to persuade the doubters.

While he lived, there was hope. Hope for the others aboard with him, hope for himself, though the hope was frail enough.

Sick at heart for Patience's terrible end, Tom left the battered fo'c'sle with the two hands of the boarding party and went aft to where the off-watch men were huddled in the saloon. He gave them the facts without glossing them over.

'The tow's parted, Mr Patience is dead. We've broached-to again, and I think we're on our own. I wouldn't expect Captain Fullbright to risk turning the ship. He'll have many things to weigh. One of them being the Diego Ramirez handy by. I don't know where we lie relative to the rocks, but I believe we have them astern and we're close enough. That's all I can tell you. Are there any questions?'

One of the men spoke up. 'What are you going to do, Mr Chatto?'

Tom made a weary, hopeless gesture with his hands. 'There's nothing anyone can do. Both of you remain below, handy for the ladder. I'll be on the poop. I'll warn you the moment we look like standing into danger from the Diego Ramirez. If we're going to hit, you'll be better off on deck. Then it'll be every man for himself. I won't even need to give the order to abandon. Understood?'

They understood well enough. There was

no complaint. But there was a suggestion. 'The bottle of brandy that came aboard, sir. Time to make short work of it, I'm thinking.'

Tom was firm. 'No. If we manage to get ashore when we hit, the brandy could be salvation. That's if we can get it ashore without breaking it. As to that...well, we'll just have to take care of it. Like a baby.'

He left the saloon and went up the ladder to the poop. The wind ripped and tore and boomed as he put his head above the hatch coaming. Holding to the lifeline he moved across the sloping deck, got a grip on a stanchion and held fast to it for his life. The wave-crests reared to either side, huge and menacing. From dead astern as he believed came, louder now, the frightening sound of seas crashing on to rock.

If that was the Diego Ramirez, they were closer, much closer than he'd thought; and, driven by the westerly gales, they hadn't a hope of avoiding them. It could be a question of minutes now. Tom yelled down the hatch:

'All on deck, and fast for your lives!'

They came up at the rush. Only seconds later the impact came. There was a tearing crash, a wholesale smashing of woodwork as the remaining mast, shivered by the sudden impact, split away and went over the side to starboard. The poop seemed to lift into the air, as though sliding up a shelving projection of the rock, then tilted sideways to rest on its port side. Tom and the others had been flung bodily from the poop, down the ladder to the waist. Tom fetched up by the wreckage of the galley deckhouse, dazed and bruised. One of the hands was screaming in evident agony, the sound coming from over the side to starboard. Painfully, scarcely knowing where he was but obeying an instinct, Tom dragged himself across the deck to the bulwarks, where he pulled himself upright. He looked over. There was a body wedged between the ship's side and a cruel-looking jag of rock. As Tom looked down in horror, the wind drove the ship deeper in. The jag penetrated the man's body under the intense pressure and the screams died away.

As Tom left the bulwarks, he found blood pouring down his left arm, oozing from beneath the torn oilskin sleeve. Weak and still dazed, he forced himself along the deck. He found the remaining men alive, lying as dazed as himself in the port scuppers. The ship was breaking up fast and the sea was encroaching, the waves driven along the deck from fo'c'sle to poop. Shouting above the howl of the gale, Tom ordered the men to lay aft with him and jump down from the poop's port side, not knowing what he was sending them into. But there was no choice. The first priority was to get away from the ship and take their chance thereafter.

That abandoning was more by slide than jump: the poop had a list by now that was little short of perpendicular. They landed in a heap, on solid rock.

Tom looked around. The night was dark but there was the faint loom from the waves, so often encountered at sea. The rock was jagged, inhospitable, frightening. Somehow they had to make their way off the spit, hope to find shelter farther from the water behind the rock itself.

Tom said, 'I'm going to move. Keep together, and follow.'

In the light of next morning's dawn they were still in a bunch, huddled in the lee of a tall rock-face, such as Tom had hoped to find. Once out of the full force of the gale, he had investigated for injuries. These were fortunately few, and only one of them serious: an arm, broken in several places, that would need urgent medical attention if the man was not to lose all use of it; besides which, gangrene would have to be watched for.

'Fat chance of a doc,' the man said bitterly. He knew as well as Tom that the Diego Ramirez were an isolated rock formation with no connection to the Chilean coast. Tom did his best to sound cheerful nevertheless.

'There'll be shipping on passage, east and west,' he said. 'I'll go and see what I can find in the way of a good vantage point and attract attention when anything comes in sight.'

'No one in his right bloody mind'll approach the Diego Ramirez, sir. Not while this weather lasts, anyway.'

'The weather won't last for ever. At the least, a ship will make a report of sighting life. It's our best hope...it's our only hope. You must all see that.'

Tom began a search, taking one man with him while the others were left with the injured seaman. They moved across a covering of scree at the foot of the rock-face, making away from the water and eventually coming round behind the sheltering face to more level ground that would carry them to the summit. Time was not on the castaways' side: food and water were of the utmost urgency. There was just a chance that a passing vessel, unable herself to approach the rocks, might find it possible to put food and water into a tarpaulin and cast it overboard in the hopes that it would drift down on to the rocks. But that was a wild hope. The chances of getting at the food even if it drifted ashore, and not past on the flow, were problematic.

A ship hove in sight distantly on that first day. Tom waved his oilskin like a maniac, shouted uselessly into the wind. He remained unseen; the ship was, wisely enough, giving the Diego Ramirez the widest possible berth.

But towards dusk the weather at last started to moderate. In that there was hope: possibly a last, flickering one.

The *Orvega* was well north now, the turn having been made into the South Pacific to steam up the Chilian coast for Puerto Montt, a destination Harrison couldn't wait to reach. The sky behind them was clear, with a brilliant dawn. Fullbright scanned the horizons through his binoculars, deep in thought. Some eight miles astern, he picked up a vessel, hull down, smoke belching from its funnels—three of them, Fullbright believed. She was steaming fast, and she had the look of a cruiser of the British Navy.

Fullbright turned to the Officer of the Watch. 'I'll signal them when they're within distance,' he said, 'and ask what the weather's like behind us...assuming they've come through from the Horn.'

Within the next half-hour, signals had been exchanged. The gale had been abating off Cape Horn when the cruiser had passed, and had continued to abate, although there was still a fairly heavy sea in the aftermath of the gale. And the cruiser Captain reported the wreckage of a windjammer hard and fast on the Diego Ramirez. No life had been sighted and there had been no reason to investigate.

Fullbright signalled his thanks. Then he strode to the engine-room voicepipe. Harrison was on the starting platform.

'Captain here, Chief. I'm sorry, but I'm going to full ahead both engines. No argument, Chief. I'll take full responsibility.'

He banged down the cover. 'Wheel fifteen degrees to port. Steady her on due south. And my compliments to the Chief Officer. I'd like to see him on the bridge. I'm going back—for any survivors.'

As before, the word spread. There was a buzz of excitement throughout the ship, among both passengers and crew. They hoped against hope that some of the men still lived, that they would not be too late. Next day the liner turned to port to head in past the Diego Ramirez and picked up the turbulence left behind by the gale but steamed on in a diminishing wind beneath a clear sky and some watery sunshine. Fullbright, conferring with his Chief Officer, had put his preparations in hand. If there should be any sign of life ashore, everything possible would be done short of hazarding his passengers and crew: Fullbright would not risk bringing his ship so close to the Diego Ramirez that she would be in danger of breaking up on the rocks. There would still be a considerable sea running.

Everyone was watching from the liner's decks. From the bridge, as he raised the

Diego Ramirez ahead on the port bow, Fullbright stared through his binoculars. As the ship came closer he picked up the figure, waving from a high point of rock.

'Someone there,' he said. 'Thank God for that!' He went to the engine-room telegraph, wrenched the handles over to Slow Ahead, then called the starting platform via the voicepipe. 'There's life ashore, Chief. Stand by for manoeuvring.'

He moved into the port wing of the bridge, called down to the Chief Officer standing by the seaboat with the boat's crew and lowerers. 'Be ready to slip, Mr Forster. I'm going in as close as possible, then it's up to the seaboat.'

'Aye, aye, sir.' The drill had been gone through; all was as ready as could be. The seaboat had been provided with a heaving line which would be used if it proved impossible for the boat to go alongside a handy sector of the rock, or to ground safely on a shelving beach. The heaving line was attached to a grass line currently lying coiled down in the bows. If the seaboat was forced to lie offshore, then the lines would be sent across and the grass line secured ashore to provide a link with the survivors.

Tom had mustered the hands as soon as the liner had been sighted moving in from westerly. He understood very well the risk that Fullbright was taking, knew that the liner could not approach too closely. It would be touch and go; but now there was at least hope.

He saw the seaboat being lowered on the falls and then pulled inshore. Heart in mouth, he waited: his own survey of the rockbound shore had told him there was no safety for a boat to touch the shore. He was able to make a guess at what Fullbright had decided. When the seaboat was within hailing distance he heard the shout from the First Officer in charge.

'I can't come any closer...can't see anywhere I can come alongside. Stand by for a heaving line.'

'All set,' Tom called back. A moment later the heaving line was seen coming across, snaking behind the weighted monkey's fist and expertly aimed. As it whizzed past him, Tom caught it and held fast.

The First Officer called again. 'Grass line to follow!'

Tom waved in acknowledgment. He heaved in on the light rope, saw the grass line being paid out behind it. With his two fit men, Tom heaved away, taking the extra weight of the grass line. When the eye had been pulled up over the rock he placed it in a fissure where the rock had split, ramming it down hard. He gave it a tug; it held, but for how long? No time to waste now. 'Into the water,' he ordered. 'Hold fast to the line, pull yourselves along towards the seaboat, all right?'

'All right, sir.'

Tom bent and assisted the injured man to his feet. 'Hold tight to me,' he said. Then, holding fast himself to the grass line, which would float on the surface, he jumped from the rocky edge. With the extra weight of the injured seaman he went deep; the icy cold of the water struck like a physical blow. Coming back up to the surface, with the injured man clinging like a sack around his neck, he pulled himself along hand over hand, while the seaboat's crew pulled astern on their oars so as to keep the grass line taut.

The distance seemed interminable. Tom gritted his teeth and hung on. When he reached the seaboat and hands reached down to grasp him and heave him over the gunwale, he was at his last gasp and could only lie, a sodden bundle, on the bottom boards.

Safe aboard the *Orvega*. Their luck had held, though Tom didn't put it down to luck: the credit was Fullbright's and the good seamanship of the boat's crew who had taken an enormous risk. After seeing the injured man taken into the doctor's care Tom was himself put under doctor's orders and sent to his bunk. Captain Fullbright came below to speak to him. Fullbright didn't waste words. 'Well done, Chatto, very well done. I'll take your full report once you're fit. No hurry.'

'I'll be all right, sir.'

'Yes, I'm sure you will, but take it easy for now.' Fullbright made for the cabin door, then turned back. 'We're heading into Puerto Montt, Chatto—you'll need to study the charts and sailing directions. It's a tricky entry—but you'll cope!'

Virtually everyone aboard had lined the rails when the survivors had been lifted on the seaboat's falls to the embarkation deck, and never mind the intense cold coming up from the southern ice. There were cheers and congratulations. Only Chief

Officer Forster hung back, his face sour as he supervised the hoisting of the boat. Jealousy bit deep; but his time would come. Before long he must be given his own ship as Master, and it was likely enough that he would command a ship in which Chatto would be First or Second Officer: the PSNC did not run all that many ships. He could wait.

There was a warm look in Grace Handley's eye as she pushed through the press of passengers to shake Tom's hand. She murmured something but he failed to catch it in the general hubbub. But when at length the liner stopped engines off Reloncavi Bay to await the tugs, she was one of those on deck to watch the ship's progress through the entry channel. Brought into harbour by Tom Chatto, she thought, while knowing quite well that in fact it would be the Captain's responsibility.

With the tugs eventually standing by ahead and astern, Fullbright rang down for slow ahead on both engines. If the Chief's wretched bearings packed up now...but the hope had to be that they would hold out for long enough.

Coming round to starboard, with the

cable party standing by on the fo'c'sle, with the anchors ready for letting go if required to bring the ship up short, a seaboat was sent away with a sounding party to report the depth of water as the ship moved in slowly behind the tug. Tug or no tug, pilot or no pilot, Fullbright would take no chances on Chilean efficiency. There was in fact a good enough depth of water; and the liner moved on easily through the narrows between Abtao and Carba Island, on to the north of the Lami Bank and then between Calbuco and Quenu Islands, a nasty-looking passage on the chart, all shoals and a tide-rip. Coming beneath the great peak of Hornopiren and moving along the north-western side of Puluqui they entered Reloncavi Bay below the island of Huar, moving into more open water. As Tom reported the cross-bearings coming on, Fullbright put his engines astern to bring his ship up, and lifted the green flag preparatory to passing the order to let go the starboard anchor. As the bearings showed the ship in position, the green flag came down and on the fo'c'sle the slip was knocked away and the brake came off the windlass. The anchor smashed down to the harbour bottom, pulling behind it the great links of the cable amid a cloud of rust-red dust.

Fullbright relaxed; so did Tom. 'Stop engines,' Fullbright said. Tom pulled back the handles of the telegraphs and the ship drifted up to her anchor. Below on the starting platform, when the telescopes showed Finished With Engines, Harrison removed his uniform cap, wiped away the sweat from his forehead, and swore without stopping for more than half a minute.

His engines had just about made it.

The engine inspection by the shore gangs was to result in a harbour period of up to three weeks—maybe more, depending on how quickly vital machine parts could be sent down from Valparaiso. All the passengers opted to leave the ship and go north by land. Ainsworth made the arrangements, guaranteeing that the Line would make good the extra expenses involved. The journey would be uncomfortable; Lady Moyra made a great fuss, but would be protected from the worst aspects by the attentions of her maid, though in all conscience Connolly would be little proof against bandits, of which Lady Moyra believed Chile to be full. Leaving behind her a volume of complaints, Lady Moyra departed with the first batch of passengers, to be carried north for six hundred miles in a horse-drawn conveyance smelling of leather and mothballs. It would be a horrid journey that would entail many overnight stops in a variety of probably filthy hovels, with fording of rivers, traversing of jungle tracks and appalling roads in a land that Lady Moyra believed to be riddled with typhoid; but it was better than remaining aboard a ship with a rude captain.

The day after the arrival in Reloncavi Bay a representative of the local police came aboard, seeking a man, who could be a passenger or could be crew, in connection with a fracas that had taken place in Buenos Aires. The Chilean police were cooperating with the Argentinian authorities and there had been telegraph communication with Valparaiso, thus confirming Patience's fears. Tom had words with them, feeling obliged to break a confidence in the interests of the ship, and after taking his written deposition they went away. It was some relief to Tom that Patience had died while back aboard a windjammer, and had died honourably. To have ended in an

Argentinian gaol would have been a slow death in itself, and in Tom's view Patience had redeemed himself.

Grace Handley was not among the first of the passengers to leave the ship. She was still there when some visitors came aboard asking to see Mr Chatto: Dolores Pontarena, with her father who, it appeared, had travelled from the Argentine to Valparaiso with the intention of meeting his daughter's possible fiancé. In Valparaiso he had been informed of the *Orvega's* deviation into Puerto Montt.

Grace Handley happened to be nearby when the Pontarenas arrived at the head of the accommodation ladder from the boat that had brought them from the shore. As Señor Pontarena gave his name to the quartermaster on duty, Grace caught the daughter's eye. Something passed between them in that momentary locking of eyes. Of course it could lie only in her imagination, but Grace felt that in some way the girl had sensed something of the facts, and could be reading into them more than had taken place. Impossible in all truth, but there it was. And Grace took care to vanish before Tom was sent for. The girl

was certainly beautiful; but Grace felt some
anxiety. She herself would not wish to have
Señor Pontarena for a father-in-law. There
was arrogance and self-importance in the
assertive face and manner. And by Grace's
estimate, the daughter was a chip off the
old block.

This Large Print Book for the Partially sighted, who cannot read normal print, is published under the auspices of

THE ULVERSCROFT FOUNDATION

Other MAGNA Mystery Titles In Large Print

WILLIAM HAGGARD
The Vendettists

C. F. ROE
Death By Fire

MARJORIE ECCLES
Cast A Cold Eye

KEITH MILES
Bullet Hole

PAULINE G. WINSLOW
A Cry In The City

DEAN KOONTZ
Watchers

KEN McCLURE
Pestilence